E.S. BAR

THESE
SANGUINE
TIDES

E.S. Barrison
www.esbarrison-author.com

Publisher's Note: This is a work of fiction. Names, characters, places, and incidents are a product of the author's imagination. Locales and public names are sometimes used for atmospheric purposes. Any resemblance to actual people, living or dead, or to businesses, companies, events, institutions, or locales is completely coincidental.

Book Layout © 2017 BookDesignTemplates.com
Cover designed by MiblArt

These Sanguine Tides/E.S. Barrison. -- 1st ed.
ISBN 979-8-9873602-1-7

Dedicated to anyone looking for an adventure without judgment and fear.

And to anyone looking for an escape.

CHAPTER ONE

Son of Fire

O n the night of the lunar eclipse, the state militia arrested my twin brother for arson. The news came with soldiers at our front door. I answered promptly to their knocking as my mother woke from her drunken stupor. When they announced his arrest, her exhaustion fled, her hands trembling as she took the decree from the soldier's hands.

Once they left, she turned to me with fire rising in her eyes. "Leena! Why weren't you with your brother!?"

"I didn't know Tristan snuck out! He didn't wake me!" I didn't meet her gaze. That was a lie. My brother did wake me, as he always did. This time, he had woken me in a flurry, mumbling something about honoring our father's death from years ago.

"Pathetic!" My mother crumpled the summons in her hand. "Fix your face and come on... we better go deal with this!"

Without looking at her, I readjusted the eyepatch on the right side of my face. It'd been almost four years since I lost my eye to a pirate who came to shore to slaughter my father. I ended up in the crosshair and, in an act of revenge, the pirate spat in my face with sizzling spit, leaving me half blind. I knew my mother blamed me for my father's death after that; if I hadn't snuck out that night to play with the barking penguins, he might have survived. So I wore my eyepatch as an ongoing reminder of my involvement.

While Tristan carried the memory of my father's dead body in his heart.

My mother snatched my arm after I finished adjusting my face, dragging me out of our two-room shack and down the rocky path toward the beach.

The black sands of my home burned even beneath the early morning sun. I tried my best to ignore the way it tore at my bare feet, focusing instead on the stone fortress that oversaw the sea. The Citadel of Janis dominated our home. From all corners of the island, the Citadel towered, taking up the entire southern coastline, where cannons practiced their anthem of shooting daily. Some days, Tristan and I would go to watch them, imagining our all-powerful Governor Pierce as she declared war on the pirates at sea.

Yet Tristan and I never approached the Citadel.

At least until my mother dragged me there with fury on her lips.

The soldiers greeted us outside the fortress. "Who goes there?"

"I have come to petition the imprisonment of the child, Tristan Davies," my mother said in one breath.

"His trial is in a week," the soldier said without flinching.

"Then let me see him."

"He's a prisoner of the state."

"I have the right to see my son," my mother said again, her voice quivering with each beat.

The soldier narrowed his eyes. "Very well. But the girl stays here."

"No! I wanna see him!" I shouted.

"Shut it, Leena. You're in enough trouble as it is." My mother let go of my hand and approached the soldier.

Once my mother disappeared and another soldier took position at the door, I stomped away, grumbling to myself. I couldn't go home; if I ventured too far, my mother would have my head. But I took the moment to walk along the path around the Citadel, keeping close to the windows so I could listen in to any conversations. I tried not to look suspicious as I walked past the soldiers marching along the sea. Multiple boats sat docked in the water, with rowboats carrying supplies to the pier on the other end of the island. In the distance, an obsidian ship captured the horizon. I couldn't help but slow my pacing, squinting at its strange beauty.

I kept my attention on it as I paced the Citadel, staying close to the wrought-iron windows of the Citadel. The ship moved like a cloud, nearing our port. As it sailed, the soldiers repeated one word: *Commeant*.

My mother's shrill voice tore my attention away from the black ship. It pooled out of the iron window a few paces from me. I couldn't see her, the window at least two heads higher than me, but I could hear her, clear as day.

"What were you thinking?!" her voice demanded.

Tristan's voice followed, quiet and uneasy. I had to hold my breath to hear him speak. "I wasn't doing anything wrong, Ma. Really, I promise. I went out to admire the sea. Leena didn't want to, so I went by myself. But while I was out, the moon turned red, and my hands started to burn. I tried to put it out in the water, but it didn't stop. So I ran, hoping to take my mind off it. But...the sound of the barking penguins' morning song startled me. I jumped, and fire exploded from my hands."

"Fire exploded from his hands?" I said to myself. It sounded preposterous... even for my brother!

My mother didn't yell. Her voice fell instead, almost a whisper. "I was worried this might happen."

"What might happen?" Tristan asked.

I could almost see my mother sighing before she said, "Your father had this magic as well. It is why the pirates killed him."

I raced back to the entrance of the Citadel after listening to my mother tell my brother a few facts about my father's magic. I knew he served in the navy, and his death came in a fight against the pirates, but with the revelation he had magic, everything made a bit more sense. The pirates might have been jealous of him...or perhaps, saw him as a threat.

My mother provided little information beyond that my father had magic.

But as I returned, I feigned ignorance as my mother returned. She didn't say a word to me as we walked back home.

And for the week that followed, she behaved as though Tristan didn't wait behind bars. Every time I dared breach the subject, she cursed and slammed the door to her bedroom, leaving me alone in our tiny shack. Yet the revelation of my father's magic continued to circle in my head. How come she never told us? Wasn't magic inherited, anyway? Wouldn't it have been better to know?

But she didn't offer any clues, only telling me not to stray from the house. So, I spent the days staring out at the sea, where the obsidian ship had docked, and the traders exchanged barrels between the boats. Freshwater, jewels, and more—each of these trades held the key to our island's success.

While I watched, I continued my wonder over one topic: why did Tristan get magic and I didn't? Magic wasn't common in Janis, unlike on the mainland in Gonvernnes. There had only been a handful of casters in Janis, and the only one I knew was an old seer who lived in a small floating shack. Now, I learned my father carried the same burden.

So why not me?

I stared at my fingers, willing fire to appear. How did Tristan do it?

Why him and not me?

The answer never came, leaving me strained with wonder by the day of Tristan's trial.

That day, my mother dressed in her best island reds, painting her lips to match her clothes. She eyed me and said, "Stay here, Leena. I don't need you snooping around."

"Will Tristan be coming home today?" I asked.

"That is a promise I cannot make."

I stayed put for a few minutes after my mother left. Once I was sure she had left, I snatched one of our half-filled canteens of water, then I snuck out of our shack. I hurried along the black sand beach toward the Citadel. I kept my head down as I walked, ignoring the commotion on the pier from the obsidian ship, as well as the calls of the merchants lining the pathways.

Soldiers skulked outside the Citadel, staunch in their uniforms, with emotionless eyes. I waited in the seagrass for a chance to sneak into the building. Tristan and I had become masters of surreptitious escapades. Surely, I could slip into the Citadel undetected.

My chance came with a man in a dark red coat. He strode forward, slicking his hair back as he walked. A group of adolescents carrying crates and barrels followed him.

Seeing my opportunity, I slipped into the back of the group. At the age of fourteen, no one would bat an eye.

If this man noticed me, he didn't show any interest.

"What are you doing here today, Mr. Hackney?" A soldier asked the man.

"My crew here needs to deliver some goods to the governor. We're heading out in the next couple of days. Would hate to forget her order."

"Aye. In and out. Ten minutes, understood?"

"Of course." The man called Mr. Hackney responded.

I followed his crew. The soldiers didn't even notice me as I entered the Citadel.

I had to contain my awe as I entered.

Opulence encapsulated the insides of the Citadel. Red and orange drapery decorated the walls. Sculptures of past governors lined the hall.

Their gaze followed as I escaped Mr. Hackney's entourage. No one ever said a word as I followed, and even as I slipped away down the hall, no one called after me.

In and out. Just like always.

So I followed the sound of a gavel to the courtroom. It echoed down the hall, past the statues, as they continued to glare at me.

A soldier sat in a chair at the end of the hallway. My heart jumped at the sight, but he didn't move. I took a few more steps forward, only to discover he had fallen asleep in the chair, mouth hanging open, drool dripping from his lips.

I restrained a giggle and slipped into the courtroom.

To my surprise, the courtroom did not have the same glamor as the rest of the Citadel. A circular room with no windows lined with benches that overlooked the stage where Governor Pierce sat at a podium. The governor glowered down from her spot, her heavy eyes and graying hair reminiscent of a storm cloud on the edge of the sea. I never feared her until that day, though. Tristan and I had run into her multiple times while out playing, and each time she bid us a good day with a smile and a bow.

In the courtroom that day, she did not seem so kind. In her black robe and bejeweled headpiece, she looked like a goddess. Her voice boomed as she spoke, her eyes focused on the chair beneath her podium.

Before her sat Tristan, looking tiny and skinny beneath the governor's stare. He'd gotten paler, the freckles on his skin visible even in the glow of the candles. His red hair, usually brighter than my orange locks, had been shaved down to a simple buzz.

My mother sat a few paces away, her arms crossed, eyes downcast.

"Show us again." Governor Pierce boomed.

Tristan fidgeted in his chair. I wanted to run over, take his hand, and stand with him in the trial. Instead, I stayed hidden in the benches, peaking around from the corners, hoping no one caught sight of me.

"Show us," the governor repeated.

Tristan held out his hands. Charred burns coated his skin, working their way up his arms. The moment he opened his fingers, a few embers of fire sat on his skin like phoenix birds in the stories our father used to tell.

I gasped.

No one heard.

The governor continued to instruct Tristan to show his powers. He couldn't do much than cast flames on his fingers, but it was enough to transfix everyone in the courtroom.

Even my mother watched in veneration.

The magic ceased with the governor's gavel. All fell silent except for the sizzling of Tristan's fire.

With a booming, resonant voice, the governor spoke. "I have made my decision. Mrs. Davies, please rise."

My mother rose, her eyes still downcast as she responded, "I am here."

"Tristan Davies?" The governor turned to my brother.

He rose, "Ay."

"As the judge, the jury, and the governor of Janis, I hereby find you guilty of arson."

I covered my mouth with both my hands to stop a cry.

Tristan bowed his head.

"That being said," the governor continued, "your magic is reminiscent of your father. So I will not give you the maximum sentence. Rather, I offer you a chance of freedom: a measly eight hundred doubloons, and you will walk free."

"Eight hundred!?!" my mother shouted.

"For damages, of course." The governor flipped through the pages before her. "He destroyed half a home with his irresponsibility. But if you cannot pay, then Tristan will pay with time. It is all up to you, Mrs. Davies."

My mother opened her mouth, then closed it again as if trying to find the words. She didn't look upset, just shocked, more or less.

Finally, when she spoke, it came as a croaking whisper. "How long do I have to pay?"

"One week," the governor replied.

"A week!?! That's not possible—I only have a hundred doubloons to my name!"

"It is the rule of law."

My mother continued to stare at the governor. Silence followed.

Then came the answer.

"I cannot pay." She turned to Tristan. "I am sorry."

Tristan stared at my mother, mouth ajar.

My stomach churned, and in an instant, I jumped up from my hiding spot and raced down the aisle. "Mama! You can't leave Tristan here!"

"Leena!" my mother shrieked. "I told you to stay home!"

"What is that child doing here?" The governor barked.

"Why're you going to leave Tristan in jail, Mama?!? You can't leave him. He's my brother. You can't! You can't!" Tears welled in my eye, and I started choking on my sobs. I hated the way it felt, like something trying to climb out of my throat.

"Leena, go home! Now!" My mother clenched her fists. "We'll talk about this later!"

"But Mama!"

"Now Leena!"

One of the statuesque soldiers came to life along the wall and approached me, placing his hand on my shoulder. I shoved the hand away and looked at Tristan. I'd never seen him so quiet. He looked paler than a cloud in the sky.

"I don't wanna lose my brother…" I whispered.

"Go home, Leena," my mother ordered one last time.

I didn't have a choice. The soldier took my arm.

And despite my cries and struggles, he led me from the courtroom and tossed me back onto the black sands of the beach.

CHAPTER TWO

An Offer from the Obsidian Ship

My mother slammed the door as she entered our shack, disappearing into the back room without a word. With a stale piece of bread and a now empty canteen of water, I slumped outside to watch the ships sailing along the shoreline. The obsidian ship still sat in the harbor, its sails glistening against the moonlight sky. It haunted the port like a ghost out at sea.

I kept my gaze locked on that ship until I fell asleep in the sand.

The thrashing of the waves woke me the next morning. My mother didn't come to find me. I blinked a few times, then adjusted the eyepatch on the right side of my face. Sand fell into my mouth. I coughed once, then with a crick in my neck and an ache in my step, I returned to our shack, dragging sand across the floor.

My mother waited for me in the kitchen, sitting at the table with a glower on her lips.

"About time."

"Sorry…"

"Just sit."

I obeyed.

My mother began, "I need you to understand. I love you and your brother immensely."

"Then why don't you give the governor what she wants?" I asked.

"We do not have the money."

"You have your pearls! And other things! We can sell the house!"

"Enough," my mother snapped. "We cannot give up our lives for your brother."

"But he'll be in jail!"

"He'll be fed. I'm sure the governor will put him into the army—"

"Tristan doesn't want to be in the army!"

"This is more complicated than you understand, Leena."

"I understand plenty!" I slammed my fists on the table, not caring about the pain shooting through my palms.

"That's enough, Leena!" my mother bellowed.

I shook my head. Tears pricked my eye.

My mother shook her head, not meeting my eye. "I'm going out. Do not follow me. Is that understood?"

I muttered.

"Leena!"

"Yes, Mother." I stared at my hands, not daring to move as my mother stormed from the house.

Never in my life had I felt so alone. Tristan was my rock, my reason, and my best friend. What was I supposed to do without him? I had to get him out. But how? There had to be a way...

I rose from the table. My mother gave up hope so fast... but I wouldn't. I hurried into her back bedroom and crawled under the bed. Tristan and I had once discovered the box under her bed where she kept all her valuable jewels. Over the years, that box had grown smaller, but inside still sat one last thing.

I pulled out her glistening black pearls from the box and stared at them in the light. Just like the obsidian ship on the horizon, the pearls changed color when the light hit them: a glimpse of blue, a smile of purple, and a reflection of red.

I knew I could sell them in the seaside market. Mother hadn't worn them in years. She wouldn't even know they were gone.

Right?

The midday sun blasted my skin, and sweat gathered on my brow as I left the shack. I squinted as I walked along the beach toward the seaside market. It was unusually busy in the market that day, with the obsidian ship casting a shadow over Janis. The patrons gathered around it, gawking in awe at its goods. Surely that ship would have the means to finance my brother's freedom. As I pushed through the crowd, I held onto that hope. Tristan would come home soon. I had to have faith in that, even if I didn't believe in much else.

In front of the obsidian ship, a man draped in a long red coat, with his hair combed back and face cleanly shaven, barked orders to his crew. I recognized him at once: I snuck into the Citadel using his crew as a guise. What was his name again? Mr. Hackney? He commanded his young crew. The oldest had to be in their early twenties, perhaps younger, while most might have been only a few years older than me. A bitter resentment echoed in my heart. What had they seen? They'd been on adventures more than I could imagine, and here they were, delivering barrels of who-knows-what to my island. It was just one mere stop on their journey. Soon, they'd be leaving for the next port, forgetting about my little island like a fish in the water.

I pushed my way to the front of the crowd, clutching my mother's pearls close to my chest. Mr. Hackney, if that was his name, chatted with a few of the patrons. He and his crew traded goods for coins, sales on their lips and money passing through hands. The main good everyone wanted was water. Freshwater had grown scarce on the Island of Janis, with only three springs on the far side of the island run by the wealthiest citizens. Once a week, as long as we paid our taxes, we could fill our barrels and canteens.

Mother was never good at paying on time.

While patrons left with barrels of water, I waited my turn with the pearls clutched to my chest for most of the early afternoon. I kept checking over my shoulder and toward my right side for my mother. If she saw me, I would be in trouble... but I had to keep waiting.

I was doing this for Tristan,

"Next!" Mr. Hackney called from his seat on a crate. Despite the sweat matting his hair, he still held an aura of command over the pier.

My knees trembled as I approached him.

He caught a glance of my pearls before I could say a word. "Ah! Black pearls!"

"Yes... yes, sir," I stammered.

"May I?"

I handed the necklace to Mr. Hackney.

He held them up to the sunlight, causing their surface to glisten with blues and purples, like the ship behind him.

"Hm. Very nice. Very nice. I can give you fifty doubloons for them."

My heart sank more. "Only fifty?"

"They're not valuable anymore. We found a whole supply of them off the coast of Jrin Ayl."

"Oh. That's not enough. I guess I'll keep them then..."

"Very well."

I took the necklace back. It wouldn't be worth selling and possibly getting in trouble with my mother if it didn't even get me close to saving Tristan.

Mr. Hackney continued watching me as I stepped back from him. His eyes lit up, and he leaned forward, staring deep into my face.

I froze. What was he doing? Why was he so close?

But Mr. Hackney answered my silent questions, "I recognize you."

"Oh—oh?" Did he see me in the Citadel?

"You're the sister of that pyromancer, aren't you? The one that was arrested? You have the same face."

"Oh, uh, yes. I'm Tristan Davies's sister... Leena." The truth poured from my mouth. Perhaps this was the chance I needed to save my brother. I knew little about Mr. Hackney or his obsidian ship. I heard the guards call it the ship of the *Commeant*, but what did that mean? Perhaps he could convince the governor to let Tristan go!

But Mr. Hackney didn't promise me Tristan's freedom. Instead, he said one statement and one alone:

"Thank you, Miss Davies. That is very good to know."

I returned home to my mother in a drunken stupor, cursing me out over her missing pearls. Even after I handed them back to her, she screamed at me for a good hour. She never hit me. But her anger bounced from the walls. She never even wore these pearls! What did it matter?

After her screaming fit, she sent me to bed without dinner, and I lay awake on the cot in the back room. Tears never came. I felt helpless; I couldn't do anything to free Tristan.

Like my mother always said, I was useless.

Mr. Hackney had no desire for the pearls; my mother saw me as a burden, and I had no special talents of my own. Tristan always helped me find confidence in who I was and what I could do, but now, without him by my side, I felt like nothing more than a child.

I wanted to have his magic. More than anything, really. He could summon fire from his hands! At least if I had his power, then I wouldn't be... nothing.

Tristan would at least be able to get me out of prison. He would have negotiated with a level head. But I couldn't even find words when a single soldier said, "good day."

I couldn't even bring myself to argue the pricing with Mr. Hackney. Tristan would have concocted a whole story about the pearls being valuable.

He would've saved me.

I couldn't save him.

And that burden kept sleep from me that night.

Even as the first glints of morning peeked through my window, I did not move. Only the knocking on the front door dragged me out of bed.

To my surprise, my mother, still cradling her bottle of rum, answered the door before I reached it.

Our guest surprised me even more.

Mr. Hackney stood in the doorway in his long coat, his smile pulling at both sides of his face.

"What do you want?" My mother snapped at him.

"Are you Mrs. Regina Davies?" Mr. Hackney asked.

"What does it matter?"

"I am here to offer you a business proposition regarding your son."

"My son is none of your business," my mother barked.

"But I am offering you a chance to free him."

"What do you mean?"

Mr. Hackney smirked, catching my gaze from the corner of the room. He winked once, then turned back to my mother. "I am a procurer of magical artifacts and individuals. I approached the governor about purchasing your son—"

"He's not for sale!" My mother interjected.

I didn't speak. Would sailing off in the obsidian ship be better than jail for Tristan? I didn't dare argue with my mother, though. One wrong word, and she might have my head!

"I know your son is not for sale. Governor Pierce did not agree with my terms. She wants your son to stay on the Island of Janis. But..." Once again, Mr. Hackney glanced in my direction, "I have another offer."

"I got nothing to sell you."

"You have a daughter."

My mouth ran dry at the statement. The room spun. Me? Mr. Hackney wanted to purchase... me? I heard about captains of ships purchasing girls and boys from the pier; they entered a life of indentured servitude, promising to stand by their acquirer's side until they hence paid their debt.

Once, soon after my father's death, Tristan and I debated jumping on a ship to seek pirates and slaughter them for dead.

But that idea soon left us like the waves of the sea.

"My daughter is worthless," my mother said as if I didn't stand right behind her.

I retreated in on myself. Nothing my mother said surprised me, but it still caused the pit in my stomach to grow.

"She has value." Mr. Hackney kept his voice level.

"Malarkey."

"Mrs. Davies," Mr. Hackney reiterated, "I am willing to offer a hefty sum for your daughter. I ask that you hear me out—this deal will not last long if you choose to ignore me."

My mother eyed me for a moment, then glanced back at Mr. Hackney, and she squeaked a single response. "How much are we talking?"

I waited in the back room for two hours while Mr. Hackney and my mother deliberated. A pit rocked my stomach. As much as I wanted to save Tristan, the idea my mother would bargain me to save his life ripped my heart in two. There had to be another way!

At first, I thought my mother would fight for me to stay. That I would be too worthless to sell—but that would be her way of saying she loved me. But since my father died, she had never even embraced me. Her humanity and love died with my father.

And now, she auctioned me like cattle.

I pressed my ear to the door, listening as each offer passed from Mr. Hackney to my mother. At first, my mother didn't budge.

Until Mr. Hackney gave a final proposal, "One thousand. That is my offer. Take it, or I shall be on my way."

I held my breath. One-thousand doubloons! I was worth more than Tristan's bail!

At least I outshone Tristan in one thing.

But my excitement tapered as I realized the true predicament at hand.

"One thousand…" my mother whispered. "Fine."

The world around me sank. My already limited vision blurred, and for a moment, I was nothing more than a leaf flittering in the wind. Nothing more.

I was nothing.

From the other side of a flimsy piece of wood, my mother bartered away my life like a worthless leaf.

And as my vision returned, I thrust open the door. The room spun as I raced forward, tears staining my eye, sweat dabbing my forehead. "Mama!"

She didn't look at me. "Leena, go back to your room."

"But—"

"Leena! Don't come out until the transaction is finished."

"I should have a say in what happens to me!"

"You have no such say! You're a child!"

"I'm fourteen!"

"You live in my house and under my rules. Now go back into your room!"

I stood my ground, glaring at my mother through tears. "But you just sold me."

"Now, Miss Davies," Mr. Hackney said as he removed a parcel from his coat pocket, "I would not call it that. Your mother is giving you a chance to live a life you never imagined. A life of the sea, of adventure, and of wealth. And with it, she'll free your brother."

My mother still didn't meet my gaze, her stare locked strictly on the parcel in Mr. Hackney's hands.

"Mama..." I begged.

"It's the best option for you, Miss Davies. Trust me." Mr. Hackney recited.

I stared at the parcel, then back at my mother. Her fingers laced around it, her bottom lip quivering without words.

I closed my eye, tears slipping down my cheek. Sure, I could have tried running...but for what? My mother made her position clear as she took the parcel in her hands.

I tried to keep my voice level as I asked the next question, "You'll use the earnings to free Tristan, right, Mama?"

My mother opened the parcel to gaze at the doubloons inside the bag.

"Mama? You'll pay Tristan's bail, right?"

"What? Yes…of course. Of course." My mother never met eyes.

Never again did she look at me.

I didn't have time to pressure her further. Mr. Hackney placed a hand on my shoulder. "Miss Davies. Go get your things. We leave now."

"Now? Can't I say goodbye?"

"Our ship leaves in the hour. Come."

"But—"

"Now."

His voice rumbled, less jovial, more commanding. I quivered at his command, and rather than arguing, I raced into my room. As I packed a few tunics, a spare eyepatch, and the wooden sword that my father got me from Gonvernnes, I pondered sneaking out the window to escape. How far would I get before he found me? Would he take the doubloons back from my mother?

But I didn't have the time to force the window open. Nor did I have the time to write a goodbye note to my brother.

I had to go. I had no choice.

Instead, after adjusting the eyepatch on my face, I removed my wooden sword and placed it on the cot. Leaving that behind would be my act of goodbye. Then Tristan would know I loved him.

That I hadn't forgotten him.

That I didn't leave by choice.

So all I had was a bag filled with clothes and nothing else. Mr. Hackney did not seem surprised by my lack of belonging when I emerged.

My mother still did not look at me.

"Are you ready?" Mr. Hackney asked.

I shook my head.

"It must be scary, I know. But you will have a good life on my ship. I promise."

"Okay." I restrained the urge to cry.

My mother still didn't glance at me, squeezing her pouch of coins, but finally acknowledged the situation. She simply said, "Behave yourself, Leena."

"I'll try. Can you tell Tristan I said goodbye?"

She took a moment to reply, "Yes."

That was the last word I heard my mother say. She didn't hug me. She didn't even really say goodbye.

My mother let a stranger lead me from our home and onto an obsidian ship without so much as saying she loved me.

CHAPTER THREE

The Sanguine Tortuga

M r. Hackney's demeanor changed with each step back to the port. He stopped talking to me, his face darkening as he strolled along, no longer bidding a "good day" to the merchants. When we arrived in port, his crew turned at once. He waved over a girl, a couple years older than me, with a saber on her hip and a bow and arrow on her back. With her round stomach and strong arms, she exuded confidence that I only dreamt of matching.

"Haritha!" Mr. Hackney called to her. "We've got a new acquisition. Get her situated."

"Ay!" She bounded over and held out her hand to me. "Welcome aboard! Name's Hari!"

I shook her hand. "Leena."

"Leena... ah! Leena! You're the sister of the pyromancer, aren't you?"

I nodded, not daring to look the girl in the eyes.

"Excellent. Call me Hari."

"Okay…" I whispered.

She continued, "Right, then come on aboard. I'll show you the ropes."

I stole a glance back at Mr. Hackney, but he had already begun walking along the pier. All that lay before me was the obsidian ship, with its black sails and condemnatory glare. Its shadow hung against the sky like a storm cloud.

"Yeah, it's a bit scary, isn't it? But it'll be okay. Once aboard, it's like any other ship." Hari smiled at me.

"I've never even been aboard a ship," I replied.

"Then you might get seasick the first night, but I promise you'll get your sea legs soon enough. C'mon. I'll help you aboard." Hari offered to help me with my bag.

I clutched it tighter.

Hari shrugged, then, with a single wave, motioned me toward the ship.

Right then, I yearned to run back home to reunite with Tristan and beg my mother for forgiveness. But I didn't run, the gaze of the obsidian ship tugging me forward, where I followed Hari onto the ship's gangway.

The gangway opened into the belly of the ship, where a menagerie of crates and barrels flooded my view. Their brown wood stained the black inside of the ship like clouds in the night sky. As I walked, even my own pale hands seemed to glow. Despite my fear, I couldn't help marveling at the sight. This ship reminded me of the stories my father used to tell about his time in the navy. How many shores had this ship traveled to in its life?

How many would I travel to now?

Perhaps my mother sold me to Mr. Hackney to give me a better life.

Perhaps she saw a future for me on this ship I would never have on shore.

But my heart continued to pound with silent sobs.

"Come on, this way!" Hari motioned me through the crates.

I followed Hari in a state of awe, taking in the hustle and bustle of the ship. Crewmembers raced past, ducking in and out of different corridors while organizing boxes and crates of food, water, and goods. So much food, so much water... and so much noise! With each step, the floor creaked. The gentle thrashing of the waves rocked the ship. A semblance of nausea worked its way up my throat, but I gulped it down, trying my best to keep my head high.

I would not vomit my first day on board.

No. That was not the impression I wanted to make.

Hari didn't notice and instead led me to the upper deck. A few crewmates shuffled about, untethering the ropes, and securing the supplies.

"Come on, let's get up here. It'll be a good way to introduce ya to the ship and all." Hari walked me across the deck to a rope ladder. She ascended it up to the crow's nest perched at the top of the ship. I followed carefully, leaving my belongings at the bottom, ignoring the way my stomach turned at the new height. I'd never been so high before, and when I reached the top, I gasped.

The eastern shoreline of Janis fledged out beneath me. I could see every single merchant in the seaside market. I could see the tiny village against the beach where my mother's home stood, and I could see the fortress that would soon release Tristan from its clutches. For once, I was on top of the world; me, Leena Davies, the daughter of a man murdered by pirates! I could take on anything.

"Welcome aboard the *Sanguine Tortuga*!" Hari exclaimed, opening her arms wide.

"The San—the what Tortuga?"

"The *Sanguine Tortuga*," Hari repeated, "that's the name of the ship."

"Oh."

"It's gonna be a lot, but I got a lot to teach you about this ship and Mr. Hackney and the *Commeant*." Hari continued beaming. "You'll fit in just fine, Leena, don't worry."

"Oh, okay…" I continued, staring out at the shore. It was all so lovely. The seas had always been a mystery. They rocked ships to sleep, brought pirates on their waves, and carried goods on their backs. The gods of the water brought storms with their anger and a calm breeze with their sighs. Would they be kind to me as we sailed away?

I said nothing else to Hari as I stared out at the island, marveling at the mountains, the Citadel, the marketplace, and even my home.

No. It wasn't my home anymore.

That was when the full gravity of my mother's decision hit me. As the ship rocked with the first anchor's release, my stomach fell. Tears filled my eye. My knees shook.

This was happening. It was no dream. No nightmare.

My mother sold me to some strange obsidian boat.

She didn't even ask what I thought. With the money waved before her, she snatched it and ran. Would she even bail Tristan out? She had to, right? She wouldn't just sell me and leave my brother to rot.

Right?

I had to put some faith in her.

The crew removed the remaining anchors, and the ship moaned with the sea.

But with the sea, my knees gave out, and I nearly toppled forward from the crow's nest.

Hari caught me and pulled me into a hug, holding me there as the *Sanguine Tortuga* sailed away from my home.

While I cried.

I didn't stop crying until well into the evening. Hari sat in the crow's nest with me until the setting sun painted the obsidian ship red.

"Come on, girly," Hari motioned, letting me blow my nose on her blouse, "I'm sure you have a hankering for food now, yeah?"

I agreed to follow her down and deep into the ship. My head hurt, partially from crying and partially from the incessant rocking of the ship. But the hunger pangs in my stomach roared louder. I didn't realize how loud they had gotten until I entered the tight galley and took a seat around the table with about fourteen acquirees. Hari introduced me to everyone, pointing at each of them as she raced through their names.

"Leena, I want you to meet Essie, Callum, Lylah, Jazmyn, Gil, Erik, Zhong, Kamalani, Lei, Lorin, Theo, Pickford, Sloan, and Wil." She exhaled as she finished the sentence. "Everyone, this is Leena. She'll be part of our crew now."

I nodded at everyone as Hari sat down on my right. On my left sat a stout, dark-toned man with thick locks, as well as a pale-faced younger boy with wide red eyes. I'd already forgotten their names. A few other acquirees glanced in my direction but said nothing, turning to their bowls of gruel thrown on the table by a curmurring chef.

"You adopted a newbie again?" The man with thick locks asked Hari.

"Hackney put her on me," Hari said as she picked up a spoon. "Just like you got Theo there."

"He didn't adopt me," the boy with red eyes muttered. "Hackney just thought Pickford could use some motherly instinct."

"That was before he knew I was a man." Pickford laughed and brushed a hand through his locks.

I looked down at my bowl of gruel and glass of water as the trio bantered like old friends. Without Tristan, I had lost a part of myself; here on this ship, I was the outcast newcomer, forced to sit in the shadows and listen.

"So, your name's Leena?" Pickford leaned across the table, grinning.

"What?"

"Your name. It's Leena?"

"Oh, um, yeah."

"Leena. Nice. I'm Pickford."

"Yeah, I heard. Is that your real name?"

Pickford laughed and shook his head, "Family name. Took it as my own, though. Don't like my first name... *Winifred.* My parents were so convinced I was a girl. They'd turn over in their graves if they saw me now." He smirked to himself and laced his hands behind his head.

"Your parents are dead?" I asked. My mind raced with every possible question to keep my thoughts off my mother and Tristan.

Pickford's smirk didn't leave. "Yeah, they died a while ago."

"Oh, I'm sorry."

"No big deal, really. It's what they get for meddling with pirates."

Pirates. The word hung for a second. Pirates killed my father. They tarnished the sea.

We all knew their stories and wore a blanket of fear.

Hari saved the conversation. "Oh, don't scare her. There are no pirates in the sea anymore, thanks to the *Commeant.*"

"Eh, there're plenty of things out there. The *Commeant* doesn't have control of the sea," Pickford argued.

The boy, Theo, grunted. "Not your stories again…"

"I'm gonna tell a story about a siren tonight. You're never gonna make me stop."

I turned my attention back to Hari, ignoring the ongoing banter. "How long have you all been with Mr. Hackney?"

"Mr. Hackney acquired us all differently and all for specific talents. I've been here since I was a little girl… he saved me from the slave trade back in Jrin Ayl after my parents died." She blinked a few times, then continued. "Saw I had a good aim and thought I'd be useful."

"A good aim?"

Hari took a piece of bread from the table and, with a single movement of her arm, sent the bread flying. It knocked over a glass of water at the far end of the table and onto the lap of a pasty young man with messy blond hair.

"Oi!" the man shouted.

"Sorry, Callum!" Hari blew him a kiss.

The man cursed and returned to his gruel, stirring it with his spoon but barely eating.

Hari chuckled to herself and winked at me.

My attention remained on the glass of water. At least we had an unlimited supply of *that* here.

Then I turned back to Hari. "Does everyone have a talent like that?"

"Mr. Hackney acquires those who are talented. Otherwise, he would not bother."

I glanced at Pickford and Theo. "So you have talents too?"

"Yah, all got 'em," Pickford said with his mouth full. He swallowed before continuing, "Damn, this gruel sucks. Wish they'd let me in the kitchen."

"Is that your talent? Cooking?"

"Nah."

"Then what is it?" I asked.

"I speak a handful of languages... all the big ones here. Obviously, I speak Delinnes, but also Vernnes, Rosadian, Jrin, Volfi..." Pickford continued to ramble off more languages I'd never heard. I'd always known my native language of Delinnes as, well, my language. It was what we spoke on the islands. I'd never heard of these other ones in my life.

I glanced at Theo. "What do you do?"

Theo shrugged, "I see things."

"What do you mean?"

"He sees the future and such," Hari said.

"Oh." I stared again at my bowl. What was so important about me then? My brother could create fire at a whim. Why did Hackney want me? It was not like I had fire like Tristan.

Well, he was in for a surprise. My skill set involved annoying my mother and completing chores.

If anything, I supposed, Mr. Hackney received a new loyal acquiree.

Nothing more.

The evening dwindled with a story time on deck, led by Pickford singing tales of sirens, dragons, succubus, and sea serpents, while taking breaks to play his harmonica. As exhaustion became my closest companion, Hari motioned me to follow her down to the small cabin that she shared with Pickford. With two extra bunks in the room, she assigned me the top bunk, and at once, I climbed in and pulled the coarse wool over my head. The ship rocked around me, shaking the beams back and forth... back and forth. I watched the lantern through a hole in the blanket, resisting the urge to cry all over again.

No. I couldn't cry. Tristan had been sent to jail, but now he was free. My mother did this for a reason.

And now I could see the world.

Pickford entered the room and undressed while babbling away to Hari in some foreign language. Part of me wondered what they talked about, their laughter fleeting. But I only felt empty. All those people in the galley had so many talents; I was left as a talentless girl... alone.

Tristan, I prayed silently, *I hope you are well and fed. I hope we will reunite again someday.*

"Ay, Leena!" Pickford called from the ground as he unraveled his chest binding. "Tomorrow, you're gonna hang out with me, okay? Gonna show you the ropes around this place. Hari would, but she's got to go be the boatswain and count the inventory and goods we got from port. I'll show you all about securing the sails and swabbing the decks... just stay close. Understood?"

"Oh. Okay…" I glanced at Hari beside Pickford.

"Pickford will take good care of you," Hari said as she ran a brush through her thick black hair. She smiled at me once, and my heart skipped a beat. Hari had to be the most stunning girl I'd seen in my life; her bronze skin glowed in the candlelight while her long nightshirt cascaded down her curves.

"Okay…" I whispered and turned away, my face burning. Her presence soothed me at least a bit.

But like a candle, even her light would go out.

Because fire always dies, especially at sea.

CHAPTER FOUR

The Changing of the Tides

Dear Tristan,

Today marks the third month of being aboard the Sanguine Tortuga. Nothing has really changed since my other letters.

Each morning, I swab the decks with Pickford and Theo, then I help prepare food in the galley. At night, my job is to secure the sails before heading to bed.

Nothing changes. I never thought traveling the seas would be this boring.

It's a shame we won't be together for our birthday soon. I'm going to miss Mother's taro tapioca cake.

I'm stuck eating fish gruel most days now.

Either way, I hope you're doing okay.

I'll write again soon.

Your sister,

Leena

I stared at the words on the page, blinking away the tears from my eye. For the past three months, I'd written these letters to Tristan. They never got easier. Not like my days aboard the *Sanguine Tortuga*.

Routine became the bane of my existence. After Pickford showed me the proper method to swab the deck and tie down the sails, nothing really changed. Mr. Hackney became only a ghost on the ship, sending orders through his crewmates to the acquirees. He never looked us in the eyes.

Unless we had something he wanted.

Some days, he called specific acquirees to his office for their so-called "gifts." I watched as he called Theo, Pickford, Hari, and even that pasty boy, Callum. But he never called me. By now, I was sure he knew I had no magic. He probably realized the poor choice he made; why bother purchasing me from my mother? Wouldn't it have been smarter to bail Tristan out of jail and drag him aboard?

Did he hate me for his poor investment?

Or did he forget I existed?

But if he did, how would I ever return home?

Home. I sealed the letter with a sigh. Whenever I closed my eye, I stood again on the shores of Janis with Tristan, laughing at the barking penguins and collecting seashells. Tristan always looked out at sea as we walked along the shore, talking about how he would one day find the pirates that killed our father and took my eye.

As I left the hull, I adjusted my eyepatch. I still didn't remember that day well. Tristan saw everything. I had snuck out of home, and at the docks, those pirates cornered me. I let out a scream, and they covered my mouth.

Everything went dark after that.

When I woke, I no longer had a right eye.

And my father was dead.

As I climbed onto the main deck, I held the letter close to my chest. The sunlight beat down on the deck of the obsidian ship, and I squinted against its rays, searching for familiar faces. Theo sat in the crow's nest, high above everyone, looking far too serious for a thirteen-year-old boy. He always had an appearance of prestige, his hair combed perfectly, his clothes dusted and smooth. In contrast, Pickford bumbled around the deck with a mop, humming an obnoxious tune in his oversized coat. His eyes lit up when he saw me.

"Ah, Miss Leena has finally crawled out of bed. Thought I'd have to drag you by your braids soon if you didn't wake."

"I was writing a letter to my brother. It's our fifteenth birthday next moon, and I hope Mr. Hackney can send it." I said.

"How many have you written now? We haven't even reached port yet," Pickford inquired.

"Five…" I stared at the letter again. "But at least Tristan will see I didn't forget about him."

"Eh, if that's what you want, so be it. Go throw it in his pile, then get your arse over here. We got work to do."

"Yes, sir!"

"Sir?" Pickford chuckled to himself. "I like that. Keep calling me that. Sir Pickford… Yes, that's perfect."

"In your dreams," I chided.

Pickford kept chuckling to himself as I walked past him toward the captain's quarters. As usual, Callum sat in front of the quarters, a watchful guard dog, sketching on a piece of paper. He narrowed his eyes at me as I approached.

"What's your problem?" I asked. Callum always had a scowl on his face and rarely spoke. He followed Mr. Hackney around the ship like a faithful pet, his coat pristine, his hair combed back behind his ears. I'm not sure if Mr. Hackney really took much notice. Callum, to him, was more of a human waste disposal. He threw papers at Callum, told him to pick up his food, and then disregarded him like nothing more than a piece of paper blowing in the wind.

"Captain's busy," Callum said as he returned to his sketch pad.

"I need to drop off my letter." I held it out to Callum, "For my brother."

"Have you not already given the captain over twelve letters to send? You realize the captain is a busy man."

"Only five..." I already felt the tears in my eye. "Please. It's almost my birthday, and I want to send this to Tristan. Please..."

Callum grunted and took the letter from me. "I'll throw it on his pile."

I didn't thank Callum, turning away without a word. *Don't cry. You're better than this. Don't cry.*

As I walked back to the deck, restraining my tears, I passed the door to the captain's quarters. No sound came from the doors. Bolted tight, blending in with the rest of the obsidian ship, Mr. Hackney's realm was nothing more than a mystery.

Like the Citadel back on Janis.

I only imagined what I would find inside his office; while I had snuck around plenty as a child, his office left my stomach raw with fright. He held this power over all of us. One wrong move... and I'd be thrown to the sharks.

Or whatever sea monster waited beneath the ship.

Pickford sang stories of monsters each night, detailing tales of sea serpents wrapping around ships, krakens tearing at the boards, and sirens leading the most fragile to their deaths. The possibilities haunted me.

As I arrived back on the deck, I heard the door of Mr. Hackney's office open behind me. I spun at once. Hari stood there, hugging herself, face puffy. Red filled the white of her eyes. Her hair, usually combed nicely, appeared disheveled. Blood stained the sleeve of her camise.

She glanced at me, then forced a smile.

"Are you okay?" I asked her.

"Oh, I've had better days. Don't worry about me now."

"Are you sure?"

"Positive. Get back to work now, okay?"

Her gaze begged me not to argue. So, I merely obeyed, glancing back once at Hari as she leaned against the wall of the ship and cried.

I didn't mention what happened with Hari to anyone. For the following weeks, I stayed quiet, performing my duties, waiting for land to appear on the horizon. I kept an eye on Hari. Some days, I noticed she would resume her usual pep in her step, a grin on her face, light in her eyes. But other days, she retreated from everyone as if trapped by her own monsters.

My routine had a few breaks in it, despite the consistency that plagued my life aboard the ship. With stories passed between crewmates, especially with Pickford telling his outlandish legends and tales, and new corners of the ship to explore, I escaped monotony. I sometimes spied on different crewmates as they flirted, escaping to the crow's nest to learn the methods of love and touch. A few times, my heart traveled with them, wondering if I would ever feel that type of enthrallment in the crow's nest.

The only time I climbed up there was not to understand love but to sit with Theo and watch the waves of the sea.

I relished this time with him, reminiscing about the days I would spend watching the water with my brother. Theo, in most cases, spoke little. He reminded me of Tristan that way. While a year younger than me, Theo had the knowledge of an old man, his eyes on constant guard. He saw so much more than I ever could imagine. When he told me stories of the stars and the sea from his home country of Delilah, I hung onto his every word.

"Where is Delilah?" I asked him one day as he finished a story about the Dueling Princess constellation.

"Far east from here, across the sea," he said, his voice flat.

"Was it nice?"

"I don't remember. I was little when we left."

"Why'd you leave?"

Theo closed his eyes. "Bad people."

"Pirates?"

"No. Pirates didn't make it to Delilah. There are bad people everywhere, and sometimes they don't like stories or magic or people who are different."

That ended the conversation. Theo made a point not to speak again, turning his attention to the deck below us. The light shone in Mr. Hackney's office, and shadows moved along the deck. Pickford continued to swab the wood, humming to himself. Callum sat on the steps to the helm, sketching pictures on his pad. He never showed them to anyone, despite Pickford's incessant demands to catch a glimpse. Then there was Hari, who sat on a barrel, her gaze locked on the sea. Theo paused when his eyes locked onto her.

"How do you like life aboard the *Sanguine Tortuga* so far?" Theo asked at last.

"Huh?"

"You've been here a few months. I'm only curious."

"Oh…" I kept my attention on the acquirees working on the deck. "It's okay. A little boring. But okay. I wish Mr. Hackney was more present, though. It would help me feel like I belong more."

Theo shook his head. "No, you don't."

"What?"

"You do not want Mr. Hackney *present*."

"Why?"

Theo glanced down at Hari again. She had shifted slightly so her head rested on her knees. "Hari knows better than anyone. She's been on this ship for nearly ten years now. Joined when she was six years old..." Theo licked his lip. "Mr. Hackney saved her from *slavery,* but I think she got the worst end of the deal. Really, we all have. Hackney owns us...and he will do what he wants to whoever he wishes."

"I'm confused. What do you mean?"

"Hackney is currently...fascinated with Hari. He enjoys her *company.*"

I sucked in my lips, my stomach dropping with the unsaid truth. If I recognized Hari's beauty at once, surely a man like Mr. Hackney did, too.

Bile rose in my throat, and I pivoted my attention back to the sea. "What about you? It sounds like you're speaking from experience."

Theo joined my side, his gaze unmoving. "It is different with me. He values my sight... and will use it, no matter the cost. I tried to avoid him at first... but it's not always possible. His anger knows no bounds." Theo paused, watching the dark shore. What did he see? With my one good eye, I only saw the closest waves, thrashing so loud they echoed in my ears. He didn't tell me, instead saying, "You're lucky he has been calm the past couple of months. But that might change by the time we get to the mainland. I guess you'll find out soon, though."

"You mean we'll be docking soon?" I squinted into the darkness.

"Yes. I see it just past the fog now. We'll be at San Joya in the morn."

CHAPTER FIVE

San Joya

I couldn't sleep that night, giddy excitement filling my stomach about our arrival in San Joya. Land! I couldn't believe we would finally be back on land! Not only that, but I was going someplace *new*. While the aching pang of my lost life remained thudding in my chest, perhaps life wouldn't be *terrible*.

I was the first out of the cabin the next morning, waking before Pickford and Hari. Giddy with excitement, I raced onto the main deck, where crewmates already bustled with barrels and boxes. Mr. Hackney made an appearance, neat and pristine, the face of a merchant once again, ready to sell wares and buy goods. He even threw a smile in my direction, although he still didn't meet my eye.

But I couldn't care less about Mr. Hackney.

Immediately, my attention turned to land.

I covered my mouth to contain my laughter.

A city composed of glass glistened at the edge of the sea. Colors danced through it like a rainbow prism from the sun. Each pane of glass cast a different colored shadow over the sea, forming pictures like a painting on the water. Even the small homes beneath the main fortress glistened with large glass windows.

This was more than glass. This city was a diamond.

"Pretty, ain't it?" Pickford came up beside me.

I didn't even flinch at his arrival. "Amazing."

"Yeah, one of my favorite places."

"You've been here before?" I asked.

"Born and raised." He winked at me. "Shame I can't get off this here boat. Luckily, Hari will take care of getting my brawn potion for me."

"Wait... what? Why can't you get off?"

"I'll be arrested, so it ain't a good idea."

"Arrest for what!?"

Pickford lowered his voice. "Would you believe me if I said murder?"

I stared at him. Was he joking? Murder!? I refused to believe it. Pickford was the friendliest person I'd met on the ship. I couldn't picture it.

It had to be a joke.

Pickford chuckled and said nothing further.

I stared back at the city. The roads glistened with metallic stones, while even the port had crystals on its pillars. The *Sanguine Tortuga* must have looked like a stain compared to all these colors; even with the colors cascading down upon us, turning our skin into the color of flowers, the ship did not change.

A whistle blew. I turned. Mr. Hackney stood on a box, holding a small metallic whistle to his lips.

Then he smiled.

A different man appeared than the one Theo painted the night before or the one who hid in his office all day. Instead, he was an entrepreneur and a gentleman, the man who I met on the shores of Janis.

"Alright, crew, we only have a couple hours here, so I want only the essential crewmates going ashore, y'hear? No one else is allowed off to lollygag. We gotta get a move on before sundown." Mr. Hackney turned to look directly at me. "Everyone else, stay aboard and get to work."

"What!?" My mouth fell. An uneasiness captured my knees and rocked me side-to-side. After all this...I wouldn't be allowed to go ashore?

"Eh, guess you're stuck here with me," Pickford remarked.

"But this is my first port!"

"Hackney doesn't give a damn. Most acquirees will have to stay here."

I glanced around frantically. Most of the crew had vanished below deck again for disembarkation, leaving the acquirees and a couple of other hands to work the ship.

Huffing, I stormed back down the ladder toward my cabin. Frustration seeped into my core. It wasn't fair! I'd been waiting for land for weeks now! Besides, I had to make sure that Mr. Hackney sent out my letters!

I stopped by a porthole as I reached the bunks. The crew had begun their arrival into port. Callum followed eagerly behind Mr. Hackney while Hari and Theo helped unload boxes. I leaned against the wall, grimacing as a headache waltzed in my head. Round and round it spun, the dance of frustration and disappointment. It started slowly, then turned faster, until at last, I sank to the floor and hugged my knees.

I wheezed.

The boxes on the floor across from me laughed and mocked in my direction. They had more rights than me! These boxes were allowed on land... Why not me?

Boxes...

An idea formed in my head, kicking out the frustrated waltz with a swaying ballad of success.

I found a box in the cargo hold, mixed in with all the goods the crew unloaded in haste. After slipping open the cover, I climbed inside, sharing space with bundles of taro root purchased from my home island of Janis. I inhaled the scent and smiled. For a minute, I was back home, eating a taro pastry with my brother, laughing about the obnoxious barking penguins outside our window.

Then the box shifted, and reality seeped in again. What if they put another box on top of this one? Would I be able to get out? And if not... what would happen if someone found out I was inside it?

Did I just make a big mistake?

But as light leaked in through the cracks and the rocking of the boat ceased beneath me, all that worry faded. I'd arrived on land. Right now, really, I could hide here forever, escape Mr. Hackney, and maybe catch a ride home to Janis. But where was *here*? I knew the city's name, but where was it? Did they even speak my language?

The crate landed on the ground with a loud thud.

"Alright then, get a move on. Got a merchant coming to trade with me." Mr. Hackney boomed right outside of my crate.

My stomach churned.

A clunk served as my greatest foe. It wasn't loud enough to be another box.

Was Mr. Hackney sitting on me? I held my breath. He would have to move, eventually. Right?

I sat in silence. Outside, the pier bustled with merchants and crewmates, but I couldn't see. Even when I pressed my eye to the small slit in the crate, I could see nothing. Darkness, loneliness…emptiness thrived. It tightened around me.

It sent me back to the day when I woke with my eye gone. The pain came first, then the realization I couldn't see. The surgeon thought I might lose my other eye, too. Even today, despite my sight adjusting, sometimes I still remembered that utter feeling of loneliness, like being trapped in the night, ignored. Nothing but a commodity.

And in this box, I wasn't worth anything more than the taro roots.

"Ah alo!" a rough voice called.

Mr. Hackney shifted on the top of the box and said, "Mr. Jimenez, I presume?"

"Yes, that's me."

"I was told you have it." Mr. Hackney's weight lifted from the box.

I exhaled, but I still couldn't move. Not yet.

"What might it be?"

"You know very well," his voice lowered, but still loud enough for me to hear. "Venom Mouth's map."

My entire body froze. *Venom Mouth*. Was that a pirate? Why did it sound so familiar?

"Ah, the map from the pirates." Mr. Jimenez cut through my thoughts.

"I've learned it made its way to you. I want it."

"Oh, what will this little map do for you?"

"For me? It will finance the ongoing operations of the *Commeant* for years."

"I don't support slave trades."

Slave trade? Sure, Mr. Hackney bought me... but I was a part of his crew now. An acquiree. I had a chance to see the world.

But... hadn't I been acquired without my consent?

Mr. Hackney growled, "The *Commeant* isn't a slave trade."

"You buy *people*. If that isn't slavery, then I don't know what is," Mr. Jimenez replied.

"I don't need the speech; I want the map."

"Not for sale."

"I'm prepared to offer you ten crates of taro, a sum of five thousand doubloons, and three barrels of fresh water."

"Now, what is an old man like me going to do with ten crates of taro?"

"It's worth a pretty penny—"

"It isn't worth much here. Find your treasure some other way."

A pause. No one spoke. Mr. Hackney's hand slammed on top of the crate.

But no words followed.

All remained quiet but for the gentle sway of the waves.

Then even the waves silenced.

My father used to tell me that the sea knows when the world is about to change. It knows when lives are about to be altered.

"I'm sorry, Mr. Jimenez. But that map belongs to me." Mr. Hackney boomed. Footsteps approached. I heard as he removed the sword from his hip, the metal sliding over the edge of his hilt.

Another beat passed.

Then, Mr. Hackney's order followed.

"Kill him."

Feet pummeled against the pier. It all happened so fast, and I couldn't see a thing.

People shouted and pushed past my crate. It rocked back and forth. I gripped one of the taro roots for dear life. What was happening? Was Mr. Hackney really killing this merchant? Were Hari and Theo safe?

"I got him, sir!" someone called.

"Bring him here."

More footsteps, then a clunk hit the top of my crate again. The wood bowed inwards.

Mr. Hackney hissed, his voice against the wood, "Last chance, Mr. Jimenez. I'd hate to kill an old man."

"You can take it from me, but it won't matter. You'll never find that treasure."

"Hmph."

Another beat passed.

Then a swoosh of a blade caught the air.

Followed by a chop reminiscent of my mother cutting raw meat.

Mr. Jimenez let out a gurgling noise, and then came a thud as his body fell.

Silence.

Until the waves gasped again and began their rhythmic song.

Like an actor returning for an encore, Mr. Hackney stepped onto my crate again, his weight bowing the boards. His voice boomed. "Let this be a warning to everyone. Do not defy the *Commeant*, do not defy the *Sanguine Tortuga*, and do not defy me. *This* is our sea. Remember that."

He stabbed the crate with his sword. It entered the wood, its bloodied blade dripping into the taro roots and nearly hitting me in the face.

I tried to cover my mouth.

But fear is mightier.

And I screamed.

Mr. Hackney dragged me back on the ship. I didn't fight it, yearning to find the safety of my ship again. The scene on the dock... It created a new vacancy in my soul. Blood pooled on the pier where the headless body of Mr. Jimenez lay. His head lay on its side next to the crate, eyes wide, mouth ajar. I stared at him for a moment, then vomited right on Mr. Hackney's shoes.

Mr. Hackney wore the blood on his uniform like it was just another jacket. He didn't seem bothered by the stains, but he showed discomfort at my vomit. At that moment, he ripped me from the ground and forced me back aboard the ship. Everyone stared at me...even Hari and Theo, where they stood by the crates. Sadness pinpointed both of their stares. Even Callum, who didn't stand right next to Mr. Hackney for once, watched in horror.

I didn't fuss as Mr. Hackney dragged me to the captain's quarters. Nor did I flinch as he threw me in a chair. I still only saw Mr. Jimenez's head, the blood, and the sword. Death, reminiscent of the pirates that raided my island, rode deep into Mr. Hackney's soul.

And I was its servant.

Mr. Hackney slammed his hands on his desk. "Why were you in that crate!?"

"I wanted to see San Joya," I mumbled.

"Look out the window! You see it now!" he shouted and pointed toward the window. "You were not put on assignment for a reason! I wanted only my experienced crew. It was for your own safety!"

"But I haven't been on land since you took me!"

"Neither have any of us! What gives you special permission to sneak off more than anyone else?"

I stared at my hand. "I'm sorry, I didn't know."

"You didn't *know*." Mr. Hackney turned his back to me. "You didn't *know*. What sort of excuse is that?"

I kept my gaze on my hands. The freckles on my fingers seemed far more interesting now.

"I have little patience for defiance on my ship, Miss Davies. So I suggest you learn to behave yourself."

I said nothing.

"But the question is, what to do with you? I could throw you in the brig... but that would benefit no one." He walked around to my side of the desk and grabbed my face. "No. That won't do any good at all. I might need you someday."

"Need me for what?" I whispered.

He brushed off the question. "No, I think the best thing to do would be to take away your shore permissions for the next year. This ship will be your home. But next time I catch you sneaking off, I might not be so kind... understood?"

"Yes, sir," I whispered.

"Now get back to work."

With my head down, I rushed from his quarters, heart racing in my chest and my head spinning from an unstable relief.

Hari stormed into our quarters a few hours later, long after the sun reached the highest point in the sky. "What were you thinking!?"

I didn't move from my bunk, eyes locked on the ceiling. No response echoed from my lips, the constant pounding of nothingness in my chest. It was like Mr. Hackney had ripped my soul out and replaced it with a blank piece of parchment. Nothing was there.

Hari's shouts didn't even cause me to flinch.

"You are so lucky that Mr. Hackney had a soft spot! He could have beaten you! He could have killed you! Or worse!" Hari's voice shook.

I still didn't respond.

"Leena…answer me!"

I rolled over so my back faced her.

"Dammit, Leena!" Hari threw a pillow in my direction. It hit me square in the face. "You are being immature! Sneaking around… acting like a child! How old are you?!"

I pushed the pillow onto the floor and glanced over my shoulder at her. She stood there, her body shaking, bottom lip quivering.

But only one question fell from my lips. "Did you participate?"

"What are you talking about?"

"The killing. Did you help kill that man?"

Hari's body stiffened. This time, she looked away from me.

That was all I needed to know.

With nothing more to say, she sat down on the lower bunk and removed her shoes. Silence lingered as she changed, replaced by the soft brushing of her hair. I wanted her to say more, to tell me this was abnormal... anything!

When she spoke, it wasn't the answer I wanted.

"We do things for Mr. Hackney, so life aboard is easier. Defying him only makes it worse for everyone."

"So you helped him kill that old man?"

"We all helped in our own ways. He told us it might be bloody."

"What did you do?" I hissed.

She sighed. "I tossed swords to the crewmates. What do you want me to say? I stood there and watched like poor Callum?"

"Well, at least someone is innocent in all this!" I shouted. "What about Theo? Is he part of it?"

"He has future sight... I am sure Mr. Hackney used it."

I groaned and rolled onto my side. What made us better than pirates if we killed innocent men?

"This is life aboard the *Sanguine Tortuga*, Leena. I'm sorry… but this won't be the first time you see blood."

My body warmed with rage. Why did I even expect morals from someone who *bought* me? I should have known it would be like this. Theo even warned me. Perhaps it was for the best that Mr. Hackney sequestered me to the ship for the foreseeable future.

Hari climbed into the bunk beneath me without another word. The sun had yet to set, but exhaustion became my new friend.

Even when Pickford swung open the door and stomped into the room, sleep drifted in front of me, soft and light like a feather.

"Welp," Pickford said, his bunk creaking as he sat down on it, "Hackney's pissed."

"Leena and I already discussed it," Hari stated.

"Nah, not because of that."

I lifted my head off the pillow to listen.

"What then?" Hari asked.

Pickford grunted, "I can't translate that map for him. It's in Yilkan. Not one of my languages, unfortunately."

I rolled over again to look at him. Blood pooled from his wide nose and into his uneven stubble.

"I assume he did not like that answer?" Hari asked.

"Not at all. Wants me to learn Yilkan right this instant, but how am I gonna do that with a map? It's got everything labeled in this text that looks nothing like anything I've seen before." Pickford tossed his shoes to the side. "How am I supposed to learn some foreign language like that? I'm not magic."

"Wonderful..." Hari murmured.

Pickford collapsed on his bunk and pulled open the curtains to the nearby porthole. A sanguine glow trickled into the room cast from the glass city of San Joya.

CHAPTER SIX

June Lok

Life changed aboard the *Sanguine Tortuga*. Mr. Hackney's malcontent reverberated through every action, and it did not falter for over a year. He stomped around the decks, and more often than not, I saw different acquirees and crewmates with bruises, black eyes, and swollen lips. I stayed clear of him, minding my duties, with my head down and eyes cast toward the sea. My excitement remained in my back pocket whenever we docked, no matter how many days we stayed in port, keeping to the main deck and out of harm's way.

No other bloody scenes ravished the ports, as far as I could tell. Mr. Hackney's shouts echoed as we docked, where he traded goods, talked with traders, and searched for information. Each port had its own beauty to it. Some stood like cities, with castles watching on the hills. Others survived as small towns, worn by the weather and the salt of the sea.

Mr. Hackney's mood never improved. From what Pickford said, he still hadn't found someone to translate the map. With each passing day, the stress grew. We had less food, and the crew didn't talk all that much anymore. Around the table below deck, the acquirees all kept their heads bowed, staring into the half-filled bowls of gruel. Even in our quarters, Hari and Pickford said little except to share a few pieces of candy they hid beneath their beds.

One blessing came out of it for Hari, at least—I hadn't seen Mr. Hackney call her to his office since the events in San Joya.

Rather, Mr. Hackney's anger landed on Pickford, his "incompetent translator," as I once heard him say. If Pickford didn't have a puffy eye, he had swollen lips. If he didn't have swollen lips, then he had a bruised neck. And if he didn't have a bruised neck, I'm sure he had wounds beneath his shirt that he hid from Hari and me.

Even Callum seemed distraught by the incident. He always stayed a good ten steps back from Mr. Hackney, a distant shadow and a quiet soldier. While Mr. Hackney never laid a hand on him, he flinched with each shout and fumbled his duties. No one was immune to Mr. Hackney's rage.

At least Theo appeared to navigate it all with ease. Perhaps it was his so-called "sight" that allowed him to anticipate each of Mr. Hackney's outbursts. I still ventured up into the crow's nest with Theo some days, and there, a sort of peace washed over me. In the crow's nest, we watched above all else.

Plus, Theo still had something that reminded me of Tristan. I only wrote one more letter to my brother, saying that there would be more gaps between all my letters. As much as I wanted to write every week, Mr. Hackney did not want to see my face or my handwriting much at all. Instead, I confided in Theo like I would my brother; both had an understanding about them, listening before talking and never raising their voices. If I had nothing to talk about, they both accepted the silence.

And there was a comfort in that.

Theo, despite his quietness, always had answers, too. He didn't always give a direct explanation, but it was better than Hari's tightlipped attitude and Pickford's nonchalance.

As the one-year anniversary of San Joya reared its head and Mr. Hackney's cursing reverberated around the ship, one question finally made its way to my lips. I hadn't thought about it, but the memory of the day dragged me down, playing moment by moment in my mind's eye. Each word returned, transporting me back to that fateful day.

I turned to Theo that night in the crow's nest. "Who's Venom Mouth?"

Theo blinked, keeping his gaze steady on the horizon, searching for whatever Mr. Hackney had asked him to find that day. I knew better than to ask what he was looking for at sea; that was between only him and Mr. Hackney.

I didn't expect Theo to answer my question.

But eventually, he said, "Where'd you hear that name?"

"In San Joya, a year ago. I forgot about it until now, though. It's a strange name."

"Most pirates have unique names." Theo leaned against the wall of the crow's nest and closed his eyes.

Pirate... I gulped. The mere word made my stomach crawl.

"Venom Mouth ruled the seas a few years back until Hackney and a few other ships in the *Commeant* killed them. It all happened just before I came aboard. Hari was part of it, though." Theo picked at his nail for a moment. "They say Venom Mouth has a hidden treasure, and that's what the map is that Hackney found. But during the battle, some of their crew disappeared with the map. Hackney has been searching for it ever since."

Was Mr. Jimenez part of Venom Mouth's crew? Or was he just stuck in the crosshairs? I didn't ask. I learned not to bring up the day in San Joya.

Instead, I asked, "Why did they call them Venom Mouth?"

Theo closed his eyes, "Venom Mouth used to attack the islands off the coast. Their main weapon wasn't their sword or crew, though. Rather, they spit venom into the eyes of their opponents, blinding them while they looted. Like a snake."

"Spit venom…" My hand went to my eyepatch.

A memory flashed before me; I was on the beach, then came the pirates. I went to flee, and one of them ambushed me. A figure approached with no sword. Only a cocky smile. They titled back their head and gargled.

And spat in my face.

That was all I remembered.

I glanced at Theo. "What does the venom do to someone's eyes?"

"I said it blinded them."

"But does it…destroy the eye? Like someone gauged it out or something?"

Theo shrugged. "Not sure. Never seen one."

With my hands trembling, I lifted my eyepatch, revealing the warped star-shaped scar. "Now you have."

Theo tried to convince me to tell Mr. Hackney about my eye. It wasn't worth my time. The events happened nearly six years earlier. I was just a minor casualty in a long list of deaths, and I highly doubted there was anything relevant about the eye burned from my skull.

When I returned to my cabin, I spent a good hour staring in the cracked mirror at the star-shaped pattern on my face. I pressed the raised scar down, searching for secrets as if it was a treasure map itself.

Nothing came of it.

Just like me.

And the *Sanguine Tortuga* kept to her routine.

Mr. Hackney's patience continued to wear thin. Even as the anniversary of Mr. Jimenez's death roared past, followed by a few weeks of anger and discontent, I didn't dare ask if I could go ashore. Instead, I moved through the motions of life but gave up on living. Even amongst the acquirees, I felt like I didn't belong. They all had talents—from magic to knowledge—while my brother might have been the only interesting thing about me.

I tried to hide the sorrow writhing through my body, keeping a light smile whenever I spoke with the others. We all had the same life aboard the ship. No one was free.

To my surprise, one crisp spring morning, Mr. Hackney called me to his office. Callum found me on deck and led me to the captain's quarters. My stomach twisted.

"What does Mr. Hackney want?" I asked, glancing once to the horizon. Land hadn't greeted us in over a week, and except for a ship bobbing on the water, the water remained calm.

"I didn't ask," Callum muttered.

I grumbled but didn't pressure Callum further. He wouldn't speak, no matter how hard I tried to convince him otherwise.

Mr. Hackney waited for me in his office, hands laced behind his back. He spoke without turning. "Thank you, Callum. You may close the door on your way out."

I held my breath as the door closed. For nearly a minute, I didn't let out a breath, waiting for Mr. Hackney to speak.

He still didn't face me. "I have finally found a use for you, Miss Davies."

"You have?" I squeaked. What did that mean?

"Yes. I ask that you stay here with me until we meet with my sister ship, the *Cobalt Hare*."

"What do you want me to do?"

"Just stand there and look pretty." Mr. Hackney turned. He hadn't shaved in days, a graying beard darkening his jawline like the circles around his hollow eyes.

My throat tightened as he strode past me and exited his office. The locks on the door clicked, leaving me once again alone.

I waited in his office for hours. From his window, the *Cobalt Hare* bobbed on the horizon, nearing us with every bounce of the waves. As it grew closer, I noticed its similarities to the *Sanguine Tortuga*. Its obsidian color reflected the blue tint of the sky, in contrast to our red, but otherwise, every part was identical.

The ships rocked in rhythm as the crew tethered them together. Other than the muffled voices, I couldn't make out what had occurred on deck. I didn't dare move, waiting until Mr. Hackney came back a couple hours later.

Two women followed in behind him: one in a captain's uniform and another the same age as me, with long black hair falling over her face. With her wrists cuffed together, her captain led her forward like a dog on a leash.

Only once did she look up, locking her eyes with mine.

I immediately looked away.

"Ms. Platt, I'd like you to meet my most recent acquiree, Leena Davies." Mr. Hackney said to the older woman. "I'm willing to offer her in exchange for Miss Lok."

"What!?" I exclaimed before I could stop myself. He wanted to get rid of me!

Ms. Platt eyed me, ignoring my outburst, "Other than speaking out of line... what can she do?"

Mr. Hackney glared at me, then said, "She is the sister of a pyromancer."

"But what can *she* do? What makes her as valuable as Miss Lok?"

"She is obedient and does her work. I've only reprimanded her once."

"Bernard, I do not want your spares and mistakes. I am sorry you spent money on a useless girl, but she is not my problem. Miss Lok here is valuable, and I have no intentions of giving her up for... *nothing*."

"I need her." Mr. Hackney argued.

The girl, Miss Lok, as they called her, did not flinch. There was a certain confidence in the way she held herself, eyes darting like a lizard as she examined the room. She kept glancing at me. I couldn't tell what she thought; was she analyzing my every move? Judging me? Or relieved I was useless, and she could stay aboard her own ship?

"Then give me something worth the trade." Ms. Platt snarled.

"I cannot trade any other acquirees. I need them. *She* is the only one up for trade." Mr. Hackney motioned to me again.

"Then no deal." Ms. Platt began to leave with her acquiree.

"If I may interrupt, I have a proposition." Miss Lok interjected. Her voice sliced through the air, poised and icy.

Ms. Platt and Mr. Hackney glowered in her direction.

She continued, voice calm and organized, "Freda, you have treated me like a barrel of waste since I first boarded. You made it clear I was more of a burden than a resource. If Bernard takes me off your hands, then you'll be free of that burden."

"I do not give charity." Ms. Platt turned back to Mr. Hackney. "I might not enjoy Miss Lok's presence on board, but she is not free."

"I did not finish, Freda. If I may," Miss Lok continued, still confident and calm.

Ms. Platt's nostrils flared, but she let Miss Lok finish.

"Acquiring Miss Davies here or any other person would place an unnecessary burden on your ship's resources. By getting rid of me, you will have one less mouth to feed. Additionally—" Miss Lok held up her finger to silence Ms. Platt before she interrupted. "When boarding, I noticed that Mr. Hackney has quite a few boxes of food and at least a dozen barrels of water. He could trade you those goods… and you will no longer have to ration your meals until you reach Bautriz in a month."

Silence followed. Mr. Hackney and Ms. Platt glowered at each other, then back at Miss Lok. Tension tightened in the air, and I swore my heart cast a chorus of audible beats, counting the seconds until an answer.

I prayed that Mr. Hackney would say yes. But why did I want to stay aboard this ship? It had done nothing for me.

But the past couple of years made it my home. Hari, Theo, and Pickford had all become my friends. Restarting aboard the Cobalt Hare would derail everything.

At least, even if I was useless, I could live. I didn't wear chains like Miss Lok did.

I had some freedom.

Or, well, more than a prisoner did.

Ms. Platt turned to Mr. Hackney, "I need ten barrels of water and five crates of food... plus five thousand doubloons."

"Five thousand?" Mr. Hackney exclaimed.

"Yes, five thousand. That is my offer."

Mr. Hackney huffed and mouthed something to himself, then shouted, "Miss Davies!"

I straightened, "Yes-Yes, sir?"

"Tell Haritha to prepare ten barrels of water then to come see me." He turned back to Ms. Platt. "You have yourself a deal, Freda."

My body shook as I found Hari, and it didn't stop even as I ventured down into my quarters. I nearly vomited but swallowed the foul taste before collapsing on the bed.

The tears I'd been holding in finally spilled. That girl... Miss Lok... she saved me. She might not have meant to, but she saved me. I couldn't leave this ship. How would Tristan find me? What about my friends?

But now I knew an undeniable truth: Mr. Hackney saw me as disposable. I really was nothing more than a pyromancer's sister. Ultimately, he might still unload me.

Another bout of nausea washed over me, but I swallowed it, hiding my head beneath my pillow as the door swung open.

"Leena!" Hari's voice rang. "Get up! I have something to tell you!"

"What?" I bellowed. My sobs caught in my throat.

Hari's footsteps approached. "Leena? What's wrong? Is everything okay?"

I covered my head with my pillow and sobbed again.

"Leena?"

"I think it's cause your Mr. Hackney tried to trade her for me." Another voice spoke.

I raised my head. Miss Lok stood in the doorway, arms crossed, eyes scanning the room. With her hands unshackled, I got a better glimpse of her. Her head almost touched the top of the doorway, with long black hair flowing behind her like a silken blanket and her dark eyes flitting about the room.

"You already met then?" Hari asked.

"I guess you can say that," Miss Lok said.

"Yes." I swallowed and asked, "Why did you negotiate for me?"

Miss Lok laughed, "I didn't negotiate for you. I negotiated for myself, so don't go getting the idea I got a soft side."

"But...you still joined Mr. Hackney's ship."

"Cause this here *Sanguine Tortuga* is exactly where I want to be. Convinced Freda to let me see the ship and convinced your captain to make a nice deal." Miss Lok leaned against the wall. "You were just means to an end."

I stared at my hands, counting the freckles to myself. As always, a means to an end; first, I was the means of my father's death. Next, the means to free my brother. And now this, the means for this girl to climb aboard our ship.

"June, you can take the top bunk. Pickford won't mind," Hari said.

Miss Lok—or June, as Hari called her—grunted a response.

Hari approached my bunk. "Leena, listen, June is going to be our new cabin mate. I expect you to help show her the ropes, okay?"

I nodded and closed my eye. At least I'd be useful for something, even if it was just for babysitting our new acquiree.

In the back of my mind, questions formed, but I had not the heart to ask them.

Time would give me the answers, but for now, I silently welcomed the newest member of the *Sanguine Tortuga,* June Lok.

CHAPTER SEVEN

Lies of the Calm Tides

June became the talk of the ship over the next couple of months. A new acquiree, sought by Mr. Hackney, always brought conversation. I didn't notice it after they acquired me, but I'm sure it happened. Everything was new and strange. Now, it became dull and familiar.

The questions around June never stopped. Why did Mr. Hackney want her? What is so special about her? June didn't humor most of the questions, keeping to herself whenever she was not with Mr. Hackney.

I prayed to myself her arrival might soothe Hackney's anger, but it only increased. June left his office each day with a bruise on her face but a determined scowl on her lips. At night, Pickford tried to get her to talk about the events, but she merely laughed, rolled over, and fell asleep.

Even I couldn't keep my eye off her. June was stunning in her own way, sauntering about the ship as if she owned it, her smile a flash of pearly white teeth. One time when she smiled, I swore I saw a hint of gold.

About three months into June's arrival and a multitude of bruises later, she ambled into the galley one evening, hands in her pockets, dark eyes scanning the room. She paused behind Callum, placed a hand on the top of his head, and pursed her lips.

Callum froze. His face paled to the point he almost looked like a ghost.

"Why do you all put up with Bernard, huh?" She asked. Her nostrils flared once.

"Mr. Hackney is our captain," Hari murmured.

"He's your slaver. Nothing else to it."

"Most of us don't have a choice but to be here."

"You always have a choice." June patted Callum's head, then circled the table. She stopped behind me.

I stiffened.

She continued, her voice like the wind in my ear, "Bernard, frankly, is a weak captain. I was on the *Cobalt Hare* for nearly three years... and Freda there was brutal. Every one of her slaves wore chains. We had no freedom, no privilege. We couldn't even go to shore." She leaned forward to whisper to me, "You're lucky I saved you."

"Yes, I know," I squeaked, "Thank you."

She patted my shoulder and moved around the table, stopping behind Theo. He didn't flinch as she leaned over him. "What is stopping all of you, with your talents and skills, from staging a mutiny, hm? Are you really that complacent? Is life really all that great? Can't you *see* a better future?" She glowered at Theo. "Hm, little seer? Can't you *see* a different option? Or do you only *see* what Bernard wants?"

Theo stared into his bowl of gruel.

"That's what I thought." June collapsed in her chair beside Pickford. No one spoke, her words hanging in the air like a cloud. Wasn't she right? Weren't we complacent in our slavery? This was not freedom. Nor was this a way to live.

The acquirees alone outnumbered Mr. Hackney's crew. But the crew had weaponry and power above ours; even with the small amount of magic held by the acquirees, it wasn't enough to overpower his forces.

And even if we could escape, then what? Would we steal the *Sanguine Tortuga* and venture home?

I'd witnessed Mr. Hackney's strength firsthand. June didn't know his power. She was still new to this crew.

Perhaps we all had her spunk at one point, but Mr. Hackney sucked us dry, leaving us nothing but obedient to him.

Or, if anything, obedient to the *Sanguine Tortuga*.

As usual, I sat with Theo in the crow's nest a few days after June's rant. Rather than staring out at sea, my attention fell on June as she swabbed the deck. She never looked at her work, always watching. If Mr. Hackney approached, they stared each other down like a hunter and its prey.

I'm not sure who was who in that scenario.

"Why does Mr. Hackney want June so badly?" I finally asked Theo. The question had been nagging me for a while. If anyone knew, it had to be Theo.

"She speaks Yilkan," Theo said without hesitating.

"You mean she can translate that map?" I have to admit, the idea of chasing after an old treasure fascinated me. It would surely be a change of pace...not that I'd see any of the profits.

"Theoretically," Theo said without flinching.

"Why theoretically?"

"Venom Mouth had a convoluted way of doing things. Even if June can read that map, it still might not make sense. What Hackney needs is one of Venom Mouth's crew." Theo squinted at the water.

I glanced back at the deck. June had vanished. Really, she wasn't like a hawk. She was an owl, soaring silently, balancing on the edge of the wind. She disappeared without a trace and watched everything with intent. To her, I was only a mouse. I needed to stay away, or I would become her prey.

I scanned the rest of the deck. Hari marched along the deck, throwing an orange in the air and catching it without flinching. As she passed Callum, she threw it in his direction. He fumbled with it, then glared. Hari's grin expanded over her face. Mr. Hackney had left her alone for quite some time now, and it reverberated through her like a new gasp of sunlight.

Pickford emerged from below deck, enthralled with peeling an orange in his hands. Did I miss the weekly shipment of fresh fruit?

I followed Theo's gaze back to the sea. A chill worked through the air, and I brought my hands close, rubbing them as if trying to produce fire. If Tristan were here, he could create a flame and warm us all. For now, I relied on friction to keep me warm.

The water remained calm, the half-moon casting a glow across the waves. Each time the wave hit the boat, it echoed a consistent rhythm.

Broken once by an inconsistent splashing.

I scanned the sea, squinting with my good eye toward the water. At first, I saw nothing but the waves. It might have been nothing more than a fish.

But then the noise struck again, consistently beating against the current.

One, two…

One, two…

One…

"Theo," I whispered, "I think someone is out there.

His attention drifted away from the moonlight and into the darkness of the water. He squinted and let out a breathy curse. Whatever he saw made him change his tune at once. With nimbleness I hadn't seen him use before, he slid down from the crow nest and toward the bell on deck.

He rang it twice.

Everyone froze.

There seemed to be an unspoken rule about what to do when the bell rang. I'd never heard it before in all my time aboard the ship, but the moment the second bell chimed, the entire deck sprang into action. The crewmates dropped their duties and immediately tore across the deck, lighting torches and casting a glow brighter than the moon. Meanwhile, the acquirees lined up against the wall, and upon catching a glance from Hari, I descended the crow's nest and joined her side.

We all turned as the door to Mr. Hackney's office opened. With his hair unkempt and saber unfurled, he rushed from his office and straight to Theo, "Mr. Barbosa, what is the meaning of this?"

"Boat off the starboard bow, sir," Theo said, confidence unwavering.

Mr. Hackney's face darkened, eyes scanning the darkness, "Haritha! Get the harpoon ready."

"Aye, sir!"

Hari left my side and hurried to the starboard bow. She removed a tarp that I never really paid attention to, revealing a barbed machine of ropes and levers. With the natural movement of a warrior, she loaded the pointed spear into the barrel. She moved with precision, scanning the darkness.

The entire ship silenced. Even the waves of the sea seemed to stop.

Patience.

A pause.

A single breath.

Then she shot the hook into the darkness.

The spear whooshed through the air.

Then, a clank of the spear hitting a nearby panel of wood.

Was it of a boat, like Theo said? Or something worse?

How big was this ship off our bow?

Hari twisted the lever of the harpoon, and as each second passed, my heartbeat grew louder. Was it pirates? Would we die?

Another beat.

The harpoon spear dragged the boat into the light of the moon.

It was nothing more than one of our small jolly boats bobbing up and down against the waves.

And waiting upon it sat none other than our June Lok.

I stayed pressed against the wall as they reeled June aboard like a fish. Once the crew harnessed the jolly boat and hoisted it up, Mr. Hackney took the lead. He yanked June from the boat by her hair. His voice pierced the silence of the ship. "You may not leave, Miss Lok."

"I believe that is up for interpretation," June chided. She didn't fight him, keeping her voice level.

"You are my property."

"So you admit you are in the slave trade business?"

A pause.

Then Mr. Hackney smacked her across the face.

The sound echoed across the boat.

Still, no one spoke.

And June didn't even flinch.

Mr. Hackney's glare continued to bear down at June. He tightened his grip on her hair, and his veins popped on his skin. "It's time for a reassignment, Miss Lok. Perhaps I have granted you too many liberties. I haven't used the brig in quite some many years, but I think you'll find it an acceptable home for your... behavior."

June did not speak, eyes dead set, calculating as always. She still didn't act like a defeated prisoner; rather, she was a predator, ready to set loose from its cage.

Mr. Hackney dragged June forward, stopping only in front of Theo, who hadn't left his spot by the bell. "Thank you for your insight, Mr. Barbosa."

"Actually," Theo spoke, his voice carrying like the sea, "I only saw her because of Leena. She heard the boat in the water."

I shrank back into the wall, willing myself to blend in with the wood. I knew Theo was trying to help. Mr. Hackney hadn't seen a use for me, so this could be my chance to shine. But I didn't want to be on June's bad side. Her dark stare scared me, and there was something commanding about her.

Upon Theo mentioning my name, her attention shot in my direction. I kept my gaze on the floor, refusing to meet her glower. But I felt it pouring through me. *I* was her next target. That much was obvious.

"Well, Miss Davies," Mr. Hackney said, "I suppose you're not so worthless after all."

I didn't reply, shrinking into the depths of the crow's nest, hiding from June's sight. Why did I care so much about what she thought? She was nothing more than a troublemaker, using the lies of the sea to hide her intention. But she also held a sort of command; June Lok was more than just a mere acquiree... and while I kept my distance, she fascinated me.

Now, she would find a reason to kill me. I knew it, without a doubt.

Then, with a heaviness in the air, Mr. Hackney led June below decks.

The rest of us sat there in silence. While the main crew returned without a flinch or a shrug, the acquirees stood there, a new weight on our shoulders, guided by the glow of the white moon. Slowly, I began walking back to the crow's nest, my heartbeat growing louder with each passing moment. I didn't even acknowledge Hari as she passed me, her face just as pale. She joined Callum by the railing, but I didn't dare join their conversation. My own worries took priority. What would she do to me if she ever escaped the brig? She certainly did not seem like someone who would let go of a grudge. Would she slit my throat? Toss me overboard?

Or something worse?

With my mind running rampant, I didn't notice as Pickford stepped out from behind the crates. His hand fell on my shoulder.

I yelped and spun to face him.

"Just me!" He grinned, then handed me a small item wrapped in foil.

I sniffed it. The scent of something sweet reached for me through the wrapping.

"What's this?" I asked.

"It's chocolate. Snuck it on board." Pickford unwrapped another piece and popped it in his mouth. "Figured you probably needed something sweet... cause I got a feeling that June's pretty bitter about the whole situation. Wouldn't want to be you right now, to be honest."

"Yeah..." I said as I unwrapped the piece, "Neither do I."

CHAPTER EIGHT

A Warm Bowl of Soup

M r. Hackney kept June locked away in the brig. He showed no signs of letting her out, venturing below decks every day to interrogate her. Sometimes, his shouts reverberated about the ship, incomprehensible and laced with slurs. But June was not offering any of the details that he needed. So life continued with the same tense sensation, bouncing up and down with the endless rocking of the waves.

Nothing changed.

The only excitement still came from Pickford's stories in the evening or his bombastic announcement over discovering Hari and Callum descending from the crow's nest. Hari didn't talk to him for a week after that. Even the waters remained calm otherwise, with no shore or ships in sight.

All the while, I kept to myself, trying to ignore the nagging sensation building in the back of my mind. Every thought brought me back to June. I remembered the darkness forming in her pupils, the betrayal on her face. She had saved me once...and now I had doomed her to the life of a prisoner. If she ever gave Mr. Hackney what he wanted, what would come next? Would he trade her to some other ship? Would he make her walk the plank?

All because of me?

The thoughts remained obnoxious at the top of my mind as I worked, scrubbing one spot on deck, watching as the water sifted in a quiet blue.

"Leena!"

I jumped. Hari approached, carrying a bowl of gruel in her hands.

"Oh, hi, Hari," I whispered, pulling the mop close.

"What are you doing?" Hari asked.

"Um...working."

"You've been mopping the same spot for quite a while. Are you alright?"

"Yeah, just letting my mind wander is all."

"Nothing on your mind?"

"Nope!" I lied. I didn't want Hari thinking that I was scared.

Hari opened her mouth as if to protest, then shook her head. After glancing over her shoulder once, she said, "Could you do me a favor?"

"Oh, um, sure."

"Could you deliver this bowl to June? Hackney asked me, but I... um..." she glanced again over her shoulder, "I have something to do."

"Oh?" I asked. I raised my eyebrows.

Hari's cheeks reddened. "I...have a date."

"A date? On this ship?"

"Shhh!"

"Who is it?" I scanned the ship. Was it Pickford? No. He didn't seem like Hari's type. But who else?

It hit me at once. "Is it Callum?"

"Shush!"

"It is him!" I laughed, "Really? Callum? Isn't he Mr. Hackney's pet?"

"There's more to him than that." She glanced over her shoulder, then back at me. "Please, can you take this for me? I'm already late, and Callum gets so particular about time and such... please!" Hari shoved the gruel into my hands.

"Fine, fine." I took the cold bowl from her.

"Keep it on the down-low, okay? Mr. Hackney wouldn't be happy."

"Of course." I grimaced to myself as Hari turned her back. As she vanished up the crow's nest, panic settled in my heart. I hadn't seen June in the week since I found her in the sea. What would she say to me? What might she do?

I inhaled twice, then strolled across the deck toward the stairwell. I kept my attention fixated on the bowl. It wreaked of rotting fish, brewed a few nights earlier. The acquirees were lucky enough to receive one-day-old gruel, but June got the leftovers of the leftovers. It was cold at this point. I would rather starve than eat this disgusting "delicacy"... but after more than a week in the brig, I suppose you might eat anything.

What if she eats me? The thought went through my head at once. Would isolation bring someone to cannibalization? No, right? She wouldn't want to taste my flesh.

That was a ridiculous thought.

But I couldn't help but create an image in my head of her leaping from the cell, pinning me to the ground, and—

I shook my head. A strange heat rose in my body at once. She would handle me with dexterity and strength. Beneath her hands, I would succumb to my death.

Or to something else entirely.

June had a sort of beauty about her that, even in the darkest nights, haunted my dreams. Her midnight hair, her sharp features, and dark eyes haunted my dreams. Now, the thought of her eating me alive churned into a quiver in my stomach. What would her hands feel like? What about her lips?

Would she rule me like she tried to rule this ship?

I shook the irrational longing away. I was more scared of June than I was of Mr. Hackney! Why would I be thinking about her like that?

Focusing on the gruel, I walked past one of the crew members into the brig. They nodded at me once before returning to their post, whittling away at a piece of wood. I kept my head up, guided forth by a single lantern over a dark jail cell in the corner of the ship.

My heart stuttered as I approached. June sat on the floor of the cell. A bandage sat over her nose, coated in red blood. Her nose piercing lay on the floor beside her. Even without seeing her eyes, I knew she watched me, unblinking and analyzing each step. Yet, despite the anger she wore as a mask, there also existed a type of fragility. She clenched her hands as if locked in prayer, while her shoulders shrunk up to her ears.

"What do you want?" She hissed as I approached.

"I brought you food," I said, trying to keep the strength in my voice. Though, I probably sounded more like a piece of creaking wood.

"Hmph."

"And, um, to apologize?"

"Is that a question?" June snapped.

"No. I want to apologize. I didn't mean for you to get caught. It's just… I heard something but didn't know what and… I'm sorry. Really." I gripped the bowl tighter.

"And I'm supposed to accept your apology because you *didn't know*? What you proved is that you are loyal to Bernard."

"I'm not loyal to Mr. Hackney!" I objected.

"Oh?"

"No! I thought there could have been pirates hiding in the darkness! Or... or a sea monster... or something! I didn't think you escaped!" My voice shook. "I didn't think it was possible to escape."

June leaned her head against the wall. "You're quite naïve, aren't you?

"I'm not—"

"You're complacent. You've accepted your fate."

"I haven't!"

"Have you ever tried to escape?"

"Yes! I snuck out of the ship in the crate once... Mr. Hackney found me, though!"

June said nothing.

"The only reason I haven't left is because I don't have anywhere else to go! Even if I escaped... I don't know how to sail or navigate or... or anything! I don't have any talents, so I'm trying to survive. Like all of us aboard this damn ship."

"Hm." I swore for a second, June smiled.

"What?"

"You cursed."

"So?"

"Oh, nothing."

I groaned and tossed the bowl of gruel into the cell. The liquid sloshed onto the floor, steam rising from the stone.

June edged toward it and pressed a finger to the liquid. Her brow furrowed. "It's hot."

"Then wait for it to cool," I grunted, then left the brig without waiting for her to speak again.

The small interaction I had with June haunted me. She never left me alone, a constant annoyance engraved in my memory. I opened a slither of my heart to June, and she paid it homage with a few irate remarks.

But why did I want to see her again? Something beckoned me to talk to her, and I volunteered over the next couple of weeks, as the moon bloated in the sky, to bring her the daily meals. Sometimes it was nothing more than a piece of stale bread. Other times, another bowl of gruel, which June marveled at as if she'd never seen a hot bowl of food in her life.

We spoke little, but the fear I had over June faded into a quiet hum. Rather, we maintained a mutual distaste for each other. June glowered at me every time I arrived, and I threw her food like to the gulls at sea. What did we have to say to each other? I locked her in the brig, and she believed me as a child.

But maybe she had been right about me. I had been complacent, at least since I tried to escape. It would have been easy to escape, too. The rowboats sat off the starboard bow of the ship, unguarded and welcome for the taking. Releasing one alone would be difficult. How did June manage herself? She had more muscle than me, but even someone as strong as Pickford needed help with the boats.

Did someone help her? If so... who?

My mind raced as I stared at the rowboats one morning. I tried to recall who had been on deck that night, but everything before June's capture had been a blur.

Just like the storm cloud smudging the blue sky in the distance.

The storm arrived at dusk.

While Mr. Hackney, Theo, and our navigator Essie generally did a decent job steering the ship clear of storms, this one extended for miles beyond our bow. We each had an assignment. Ready the sails, secure the goods, and brace for impact; as long as the ship kept moving and the *Sanguine Tortuga*'s strong hull remained upright, we could survive this storm and darkest nights. With Theo's sight, we prepared before the clouds arrived, raising heavier sails and securing the deck.

But even with a future bit of knowledge, the storm came with a vengeance.

Mr. Hackney screamed over the rain for us to tie down the rest of the goods. Hari repeated his orders, her hair drenched against her face, eyes bugging from her head. Callum followed her with his own hair plastered to his forehead.

With each gust of wind, my nerves heightened. I occupied myself by tying down more crates, but with each thrashing wave and explosion of salt water onto the deck, nausea and unease climbed into my heart. Would the boat tip over in the water? Would I ever know the feeling of warm, dry clothes again? A storm on land was one thing, a gentle rain on the boat was another, but this storm was a monster, ready to stop the *Sanguine Tortuga* in its track.

"Theo! Get the hell down from there!" Hari shouted up to the crow's nest as she, Pickford, and I finished tying down a crate.

"Don't make me come get ya, boy!" Pickford added.

"Coming!" Theo clamored down, one wrung at a time, the wind battering his body. His legs flapped like flags in the wind. He spoke as soon as he landed on the deck of the ship. "We'll be in this thing for three hours if we keep our trajectory northwest."

"How long if we go south?" Hari asked.

"I'd say five."

"I'll let Mr. Hackney and Essie know. But the four of you need to get below decks. Make sure everything is tied down. If we lose anything, Mr. Hackney's going to throw us overboard."

"Aye, *Captain*!" Pickford mocked.

Hari rolled her eyes at him, then rushed through the bellowing rain toward the captain's cabin.

An exhale of relief escaped my lips, and without waiting for any further confirmation, I moved to the stairwell through the blinding rain. Below deck would be dry and safe. If my life ended, at least the last thing I saw wouldn't be the anger of the waves.

Still squinting from the bombardment of water, I navigated down the stairwell using my hands. If anyone followed, I couldn't hear them over the roaring of the storm.

The dim lights below deck beckoned me like the rising sun. I laughed as the door closed behind me and sank between the boxes. My body shook. From the cold or from fear? I wasn't sure. The storm had only just begun. All the while, the ship rocked side to side, teetering on a dance of washed ashore stories. If this ended the *Sanguine Tortuga*, would we be like those legends whispered in port that Tristan and I listened to while sneaking out of the home?

Would we be nothing more but a song on the sea?

Empty. Bloodied.

Dead.

I inhaled once. No. I would not become some storyteller's tale. We would survive.

There was nothing to fear on these seas. A storm would not destroy the *Sanguine Tortuga*.

I muttered these words like a prayer, rubbing my upper arms with my hands for warmth. The chills stopped, and a gentle heat filled my empty hiding spot. Alone, at least I had a moment to breathe.

At least—

Footsteps approached. I picked my head up from my knees and glanced above the crates. No one loitered amongst the boxes.

Another gust of wind rocked the boat before I called out. The crates creaked.

Then I felt it, right on my neck. A cold blade pricking the center of my back.

With it came a voice, the voice I knew well by now.

The one that haunted my sleep. *June's* voice.

"Now, Leena, you're going to help me. You understand?"

CHAPTER NINE

Fire at Sea

I held my hands up over my head as June led me deep into the belly of the ship. The boat continued to rock, and with each bobbing of the ocean, her dagger bounced up and down on my skin. I winced but didn't fight it. Now, part of those disturbing dreams might just come true if I let them; she would pin me down against the ground, bring her dagger close, and skin me alive.

"In here," June hissed, pushing me into a storage room hidden within the boxes. I ducked beneath the doorframe into a dimly lit room.

My stomach dropped.

Hari and Pickford sat on two crates, snacking away on pieces of chocolate.

My mouth went dry. "What… what are you—what's going on?"

June released me as she spoke. "What does it look like? We're gonna put Bernard in his place."

"What... what?" I turned to Hari. "What's going on, Hari?! Really?"

Hari hopped off the crate, "Now, Leena, I wanted to tell you but—"

"But what?! I couldn't be trusted?"

"Exactly!" June said as she leaned against the wall.

"But—" My throat tightened.

"Listen, Leena, please." Hari approached me, but I shied away from her. "Please. I trust you. Pickford trusts you. But June didn't, and this is her plan."

"And you did notice the boat," Pickford added.

"But I didn't know it was June! I can't even see well... How was I supposed to know?" My entire body rocked, tension continuing its ugly mount in my chest. *Don't cry. Don't cry... please don't cry.*

"Yeah, you established that," June muttered as she picked at her nails. "But I didn't have a reason to include you in this debauchery 'til recently. Wanted to keep my loyal crew small."

"Wait...there are others involved?"

"Only us and Theo," Pickford said.

My head spun. I brought it to my knees and exhaled hard. All my friends kept me out of this.

"If it makes you feel any better, I haven't told Callum," Hari said.

"Oh, that makes me feel *tons* better!" I snapped. "It's good to know I had no use for all of you until recently. And what *is* that use now, anyway? Am I good at bringing you things... or *listening* to the sea? Do you just want to use me as a decoy or something? Don't you understand? I *don't* have any talents! Mr. Hackney has made that clear!"

June hopped off the crate and grabbed the torch from the wall. She stared at the flame, then approached me.

I remembered Hari's screams first.

Then Pickford's protests.

Then I realized June grabbed my hand and stuck it into the center of the torch flame.

I opened my mouth to shriek.

But stopped.

I felt no pain.

In fact, the flame didn't even touch my skin. Rather, it hovered over it, like a gull sailing over the sea. As I moved my fingers, the flames danced with them. One finger and the flames shortened; two and they expanded. When I wiggled my fingers, the flames seemed to bounce between each.

June pulled the torch away, smirking. The flames remained above my hand, filling the room with a pulsing glow.

"What's happening?" I asked, staring into the fire.

"You tell me," June replied.

I continued to bounce the fire between my fingers. Did I inherit the same magic as Tristan?

"My brother was arrested for arson... for magic... " I whispered as I closed my palm over the flame. "I didn't think I had the same talent. Mr. Hackney acquired me initially because of my brother. I guess... he knew what he was doing."

June smiled. It was brief, but she smiled nonetheless. "Glad my intuition was correct."

"How did you know?" I closed my fist and the flame, to my amazement, died.

"The food you delivered was hot. It's never hot. Assumed it was your doing."

"What if I was just being nice?"

"Were you?" June raised her eyebrows.

"Uh... no."

"Exactly." June winked.

I flushed and looked at my hands.

"Now that we got all that out of the way... " June kicked her feet up on the crate. "Let's get this plan in motion."

In the heart of this hidden cupboard, I learned everything June had been up to the past few months. Since June had climbed on board, she'd slowly been recruiting her "crew." Hari had been the first she snagged—with perfect aim and distaste against Mr. Hackney. She was a clear patron. Soon followed Pickford, the strength and sneak of the operation. They were the initial two members of the crew, and they helped June plan the first escape. Pickford helped Hari onto the boat, using what he called his "cunning charm" to woo the guards. They knew the risks, though. Hari told June that if Mr. Hackney discovered her, then she wouldn't be able to miss. It would be too obvious—she'd never missed before in her life.

June recruited Theo after the failed escape, and with his all-seeing sight, he devised a lie to our navigator Essie that there was no way to avoid it. She didn't suspect a thing.

Meanwhile, everything else came into motion. It turned out all those meals I'd been delivering to June contained different keys that Pickford had snagged off different crewmates. She tested the locks at night, methodical in her deceit, until finally finding the correct key three nights earlier.

The storm provided perfect coverage for the escape. No one would check the brig while manning the decks.

Initially, Pickford was supposed to lead me into this small crevasse for June to confront me... but I wandered off before he could corner me. June decided it would be more fun to ambush me, which I griped about for a good three minutes.

June kept most of the plan close to her chest as she pushed aside a crate. In her escape, she'd gathered a few weapons. On her hip, she bore a set of daggers, and behind the crate sat a bow and arrow, a cutlass, and a broadsword. Hari gravitated toward the bow and arrow, leaving Pickford and me staring at the two swords.

"Leena, you probably want the cutlass. Lighter in weight." June muttered as she spun one of her daggers around in her hand.

I lifted the cutlass and weighed it in my hand. My fingers trembled as I secured it on my hip. I'd never held a sword before, but June didn't spare a moment to discuss training. She moved straight into passing the broadsword to Pickford, continuing her undetailed layout of the plan.

"We're gonna take 'em by surprise. Take each formal crew member and lock 'em up, eat the key or throw it overboard—I don't give a damn." June spun her dagger in her hand. "Once the storm clears, Leena...you can take on Bernard."

"Wait...what?" I stammered.

"You got the best offensive magic here. Don't worry. We'll be right on your tail."

"But I don't even know how to control the fire! I... This is a lot. Can't we...can't I practice a bit?"

"We don't have the time. We'll be exiting the storm in an hour or so. Just trust us. And if it doesn't work, we'll be ready to attack."

I started to say something, but Pickford cut me off instead. "Wait a minute here! I thought we were just escaping!"

"I have bigger fish to fry." June patted Pickford's cheek and approached the door. "Now come on. The storm will not last forever."

We split into two groups. Hari and Pickford went their own way to derail parts of the crew while June babysat me. She still bore down on me, judging each of my movements, hissing each time I stepped too loudly. I didn't know what to do as we walked through the halls. June would lead, and I would be nothing more than her loyal follower.

My hands warmed as I gripped the hilt of my cutlass. Now that I knew what I could do, I was more aware of the heat in my hands. Had they always done this? Was this why I seldom felt cold? If only I could ask my father! But even when I thought of my father, I only envisioned Tristan. Had he learned everything about his magic over the past three years? Could he tame it with a flick of his fingers?

As we continued walking, even the candles flickered with my movement. The flames reached for me, begging to be part of my skin. I could only hope that it would come when I called it.

But did I have the heart to attack Mr. Hackney?

Every time footsteps approached, June would disappear into the shadows. She'd tug my hair back as she disappeared, pulling me hard against the wall. If the footsteps belonged to another acquiree, I'd loosen my grip around the sword. But if it were a crewmate, my grip tightened.

And June conducted her own form of magic.

She leapt from the shadows, nimble as a spider, and wove around each crewmate. With a dagger in hand, she pinned them to the wall.

The first few crewmates surrendered with merely a heavy whack to the head. They crumbled down, and June kicked them three times more until blood bubbled from their mouth.

I suppressed the urge to scream.

June said nothing with a final grunt and a kick. Despite her slender stature, she had the strength of some of the biggest crewmates on board. She took them down with ease—at least at first.

By the fourth crewmate, June's bloodthirst sifted through her demeanor. The crewmate—a large fellow with two sabers on his hip—swung as June lunged toward him and sent her flying. She landed in the stairwell mere inches from me. Without getting off the ground, she removed one of her daggers and threw it straight at the crewmate. It missed him by a hair.

While he recuperated, June snatched the cutlass off my hip and lunged at him. She worked the cutlass like an extension of her arm and, in one movement, sliced open the crewmate's neck.

The crewmate stumbled backward, holding his throat as the blood gushed from the wound. He hit the ground with a gurgle.

Then silence.

June replaced my cutlass as I gawked. For a moment, my mind traveled back to the day in San Joya. Blood poured over my vision.

That was a single death.

How many more would happen this evening?

I gagged, turned away from June, and upchucked in the corner. Everything twisted around me, but I swallowed back the remaining nausea to pursue June.

As June moved, it was like the sun on rising the horizon. She walked through the blood, unphased as she picked her daggers off the floor. As she passed her victim, she kicked his body once, then, with a wave of her hand, beckoned me to follow.

"June!" I hissed after her. "I didn't sign up for mur-der!"

"You're only reclaiming what was stolen from you," June muttered as we reached the stairwell.

"What?"

"Your life, Leena. Bernard and all these other *acquirers* steal your freedom and your life. They are only getting what they deserve." She glared back at me. "If you don't want a part in this, the jolly boats are off the starboard bow."

I considered for a moment. If I escaped via rowboat, I would be free of the repercussions of this excursion. But I doubted I could row for longer than an hour.

So I shook away the idea and continued following June along the red-stained hallway.

Blood continued to reign as we ascended the ship. June would attack with a thirst for a kill. Some she left un-conscious on the ground, while others she carved like a piece of wood, removing eyes and tongues.

Like a pirate.

My head ached with each of her brutal decisions, bringing me back to a flood of red on the shore of Janis.

The scar beneath my eyepatch twitched.

If I did this, was I any better than the pirates who took my eye?

While I could have helped, June thrived on each attack. It was as if the blood brought her to life.

And I felt small and weak in her presence.

But as I watched her kill, and my horror grew less powerful, I had to admire the beauty in her attack. Each movement came like the sway of a dance; she was a dancer, a performer, and, perhaps in her mind, at least, a queen.

My head spun from her splendor while my stomach ached with disgust. My heart, head, and body argued with each other as we reached the stairs to the main deck.

"Are you ready, Leena?" June whispered.

"No..." I said.

"Ah, well, too bad. It's time for action."

"I still don't know what to do, though."

"Eh, I have faith you'll figure it out."

June hoisted open the door to the main deck and stuck her head out. The rain had finally stopped, leaving a taste of saltwater loitering in the air. I inhaled once, washing away the scent of iron and blood. If I closed my eye, I might wake up in my cabin without blood on my pants or burns on my hands.

But when I exhaled, I still stood behind June, climbing the ladder out onto the main deck.

Darkness greeted me as we climbed on deck, making it even more difficult to see. Specks of rain dotted my skin, remnants of the last few clouds drifting along the horizon. In the sky, casting its bloody glow, watched the red moon.

Pausing for a moment, I took in its red aura.

It told a story and a promise: this night would forever bask in blood.

I gulped and reached for the handle of my cutlass. Warmth filled the palms of my hand. I had no clue how to summon fire, and now June expected me to be the hero today? Did she expect me to *kill* Mr. Hackney like she had so ruthlessly done to the others?

I eyed June as she strode forward, undeterred by the silence on deck. She held her daggers at her side, dripping with blood. She wore it naturally as if the blood belonged on her skin and nowhere else. Where did she come from that death came so naturally? What fueled the rage deep in her core?

I had no answers.

Instead, everything remained silent. Even the sea.

June beckoned me forward, attention on the captain's cabin. She threw a single dagger without flinching as a crewmate descended from the crow's nest. The blade hit the crewmate in the leg, and they cried out in pain.

Thank goodness it wasn't Theo.

June kept her stride, vanishing in and out of the light from the moon. I kept losing track of her, and with every step, I grew more faint. We had killed people! And now...

we were going after Mr. Hackney? This was preposterous! All of it had happened in a mere blink of an eye, and I stood on deck, committing treason to my captain.

No. Not my captain.

My enslaver.

I had to remember that he was nothing more than my enslaver. I could never leave; he bought me because he saw something in me.

Did he know I had fire? Was he frustrated because I had never ignited?

As my head spun, June vanished into the darkness of the ship again. The main deck stretched out in front of me. Was it always that big? During the day, the ship felt so small… but now…

Something tugged on my hair. I fell backward, dropping my cutlass at my side as a figure stepped out of the shadows and pulled me up by my neck.

Mr. Hackney glowered at me, his hair uncombed, his eyes inflamed with rage. His hand tightened around my throat.

I struggled against him, tearing at his fingers. They didn't budge. My breathing argued with my gasps, unable to escape. And with it, everything slowed. The silence echoed. Was this it? I should have known; the taste of freedom was far too sweet, and I was not ready to devour it. I would die aboard this ship.

I would never see my brother again.

Spots filled my vision. His rough hands tightened.

I would never go home.

My mouth tasted of blood.

This was it.

"Leena!" someone shouted. "NOW!"

That single statement, that single word, it gave me enough momentum to force my hands forward. I flailed, my focus on the center of my palms as I grabbed Mr. Hackney's hands.

I wish I knew what caused my magic to spark. Whether it was by the power of June's voice, the angry glare of the moon above, or my own fear, heat mounted in my palms.

Mr. Hackney yelled and dropped me to the ground.

I rolled over, a gasp of fire escaping my fingers as I pulled myself from the ground, heaving. Mr. Hackney held his scorched wrists and hands against his chest, fury brimming in his chest. Another breath heaved from my chest, and with it, I breathed a gasp of fire.

It puffed through the air, like the breath of some dragon, and flew straight over Mr. Hackney's head, setting his hair ablaze.

He stumbled backward, screaming. Each step took another heartbeat.

One, two...

One, two…

One…

Smoke gathered from the flames. I didn't know how to stop it. If the fire caught the wood… then…

My thought never finished as June lunged from the smoke at Mr. Hackney. She bore my cutlass in her hand, and as she cornered Mr. Hackney at the edge of the boat, she bore the confidence of a captain.

There she stood before him, eye-to-eye. For the first time, I saw true fear in Mr. Hackney's eyes. Not when I set his hair ablaze; not when I burned his hands.

But when he stood there, facing June Lok, his body shrank.

Then, everything broke.

June took the cutlass and, with the tip of the sword, pushed him over the railing and into the water.

There, his body hit the water like solid ground and disappeared into the abyss of the sea.

CHAPTER TEN

The New Captain

I slumped back to my cabin. Embers danced on my burned fingertips, and my mouth tingled. Blood trailed along my feet. The ship wreaked of death.

While all fell silent.

I didn't care what happened after Mr. Hackney fell into the water. The moment he disappeared, I darted from the sea.

Alone now, I collapsed on the floor of the cabin and sobbed.

What had just happened? I stared at my shaking hands. The last embers flared out over my fingertips, leaving me in the dark.

How did any of this make me better than the pirates who killed my father? I stood idly by as June slaughtered...how many people? I lost count. The deaths blended together, a conglomerate of empty stares, all asking the same confounding question: why?

That was the question, wasn't it? *Why?* Could we have done this without bloodshed? Why did I even agree to this in the first place!? It wasn't like Mr. Hackney ever did anything *that* bad to me.

To me.

That was the phrase, wasn't it? To me? I'd seen what he'd done to Hari and to Pickford. And of course, I had a front-row seat to him slaughtering Mr. Jimenez. Who was to say I wouldn't be next?

To me.

Now, though, was I any better?

The door creaked open. "Leena?"

I didn't lift my head.

The door opened more. Hari walked in, blood staining her camise. She joined my side.

For a time, neither of us spoke. Hari bowed her head as if in prayer, then brought her hands to her chest.

I didn't move.

Until Hari raised her head again and said, "I should have warned you…"

"About what?"

"All of this."

"You knew June would kill?"

"I knew to escape Hackney, we all had to kill." Hari sighed. "I've known—knew Mr. Hackney long enough to realize he wouldn't go down without a fight. I've seen countless pirates board this ship, and he'll stand against it on the brink of death... fighting until the last ones leave. It was either kill him... or remain his property."

"Doesn't this make us the same as pirates, though?" I asked, not meeting Hari's gaze.

"What is pirate but a name given to the outlaws by those in power?"

"They're murders."

"So is Mr. Hackney."

"I only saw him murder once—"

"You were lucky. I've seen him murder many more."

Theo had said the same thing.

I licked my lip, then said, "So you knew June was... like that? A... a murderer?"

Hari picked up my coat from the floor and folded it, not looking at me.

"Please, Hari. I feel like everyone knows what's going on except me."

She placed my coat on the bed. "I don't know much. I can promise that. But understand, June is no stranger to blood, and there are rumors about her whispered throughout the sea."

"Like what?"

"That she's the daughter of a pirate."

Nausea rippled through my stomach. The words quivered on my lips as I asked, "Venom Mouth?"

Hari nodded. "Ay. Venom Mouth."

I stayed in bed until morning came. Sleep came in a few winks. Whenever I closed my eye, I only saw blood and fire. Every thirty minutes, I woke in a sweat, heat welling in the palms of my hand and my head pounding. If I let my sleep get the best of me, might I set the entire cabin ablaze?

When the sun rose, June summoned everyone to the main deck. With my head bowed and my hands clenched, I kept toward the back of the crowd. I didn't want people to know I'd been involved with the deaths staining the obsidian ship.

I didn't want to remember either.

A little over half of Mr. Hackney's crew sat in shackles around the crow's nest. Some of them I recognized from the night before, with bruised faces, missing eyes, and bloodied wounds. June paced before them, one of Mr. Hackney's hats on her head, a swagger in her step. She moved like a pirate. At least, how I pictured a pirate moving. She bore confidence, and when she threw her head back in a laugh, I swore it cut through the air like a knife.

"Listen here," she turned to the group of acquirees standing before her, "This is our ship now. But I'm not gonna force any of you to stay. But if you stay, I expect loyalty. I expect honesty. And I expect obedience. If you can't give me that, then I'll deposit you when we make landfall in two days. Got it?"

Murmurs followed in the crowd. Everyone had witnessed the bloodshed; we all had to decide. We either joined June for a life of crime or abandoned the *Sanguine Tortuga* for life in an unknown city.

Neither sounded appealing.

But even if I could leave and find myself a way home, would they welcome back a pirate?

"Leena!"

I jumped. I didn't see June come up beside me. Hari and Pickford followed behind her.

"Need you with us. Come on."

"I—"

"Come on, girl." June took my arm and dragged me away from the commotion. Groups of acquirees had come together, discussing with their heads bowed the events. Callum sat alone on a box, staring at the sea. He stole a quick glance in Hari's direction.

June ushered us into what used to be Mr. Hackney's cabin and collapsed behind his deck. Theo already waited in the room, staring hard at a cabinet, tracing the edge of the lock with his finger. He didn't budge as we entered.

"Well, guess we got this ship here now, don't we?" June kicked her shoes up on the desk and smirked at us.

I squirmed. No one spoke.

"Come on now, get excited. We defeated the prick, Bernard. He won't bother us again."

I glanced at Hari.

As always, she had the voice to speak, "It will take time, June—erm, Captain."

"Just call me June. We're not about those formalities here."

"Right, June." Hari glanced at me, then back at our new captain. "What I meant is... some of us haven't experienced death like that before. We'll be able to celebrate once the initial shock passes."

"Hmph." June's attention focused on the door, "Well, I hope not too long. We have work to do."

None of us replied. Even Pickford, who usually bore such a large smile on his face, seemed distracted.

We now ran this ship.

Well, June did. But we were her crew.

Not acquirees.

A crew.

"What are we going to do now?" I finally asked.

June smirked and leaned toward me. "Once we get this crew sorted, we do what we gotta do. Theo's working on getting Bernard's cabinet here open, and we can see what plans he had in store. Might as well collect a nice fortune while we're at it."

"But what if people don't stay?" Pickford asked.

"We don't need a big crew. Just enough to manage." She sat up slightly. "Just got to find people we trust. Though, not sure how I feel about some of these pricks."

"Like who?" Hari asked.

"Well, that Callum fellow. What's with him?"

"He can be trusted."

"I'd rather hear from someone other than you. It's no secret what the two of you do in the Crow's Nest."

Hari flushed.

Theo spoke from his spot by the cabinet, not bothering to turn around to face us. "Callum might be a bootlicker, but he only followed Hackney around because that's what he knows. Did it for survival's sake."

"You and Callum are chums?" Pickford asked.

"We weren't." Theo poked at the cabinet, returning to his intense investigation of the locking mechanism.

"Right. Monitor him." June picked at her nails. "What about the navigator?"

"Essie will join us," Pickford responded.

"How about Wil?"

June continued to rattle off different names of crewmates. Despite being called into this room, I was nothing more than a fly on the wall. June used me as a weapon, nothing more. Did I even belong on this ship?

How could I be loyal to a pirate? And not just any pirate, but the daughter of the one who killed my father? The thought caused my palms to warm, and I pushed it back with a gulp. This magic scared me. No one here understood the repercussions of it. What if I set the whole ship ablaze? What if I hurt someone? What would happen if the fire didn't stop?

I always wanted to be special, but this was too much.

Did Tristan feel this way when he discovered his fire? Or did he accept his magic with a content stride?

"Leena, I said you're dismissed." June's voice cut open my thoughts. Hari and Pickford had already left the room while Theo continued to work away on the cabinet. I withdrew from the rest of the conversation, my head spinning.

"Oh, sorry," I turned, then paused, glancing back at June. Her staid expression glowered over me. My nerves gathered in my stomach as I spoke. "Can I ask a question?"

"If you must."

"Where do you come from? Why did it matter to take this ship?"

June smirked and leaned back in her chair. "I come from freedom."

"We all came from freedom at some point."

"Hmph."

"Answer me."

"Be more direct, and I will."

My anger boiled, but I kept the heat in tow. "Are you a pirate?"

June raised her head. "We all are pirates now."

"You know what I mean!"

"Do I?"

I cursed beneath my breath, then asked, "Were you a pirate before taking the *Sanguine Tortuga*?"

June continued that ridiculous smile. "What is a pirate but a name?"

"Dammit! Hari said the same thing! Give me an answer!" I screamed. Warmth raised in my hands, and before I could control it, a small ball of fire erupted from my palms. It shot across the room, setting the cabinet ablaze just above Theo's head. He leapt up, acting quick to dampen the flames.

June didn't flinch, glancing over her shoulder as Theo put out the fire. It left a big enough hole in the cabinet to reach inside the fixture. "I suppose that is one way to open the cabinet. We will need to work on controlling that flame, though."

I stepped back from her. "We won't work on anything."

June hadn't heard me. Or if she did, she didn't react. Instead, she moved Theo to the side and reached inside the hole, unlocking the cabinet and letting the door swing open. She didn't even take time to examine the insides, reaching directly for a single piece of parchment stored in the bottom drawer.

The parchment, ravaged by years of wear and tear, unfolded on the desk as if begging for a set of eyes. Etchings of continents, islands, and currents greeted me. Along the coastlines, words in an unfamiliar language marked the page.

But only one thing caught my eye.

A small, star-shaped ink smudge sat in the corner of the map. Indiscrete, almost hidden by the rest of the map, no one noticed it.

Well, except me.

"Been waiting to get my hands on this for years," June whispered.

"Because you're Venom Mouth's daughter?" I asked.

"Hm?"

"You heard me," I said. "That map belonged to Venom Mouth. You wanted it back."

June stared back at the paper and said nothing.

That was the only answer I needed.

Without another word, I left the captain's quarters. Whatever plans June had in store for me, I wouldn't be part of it.

Even if she was the new captain, even if I joined in her frivolities, this was not the life for me.

I would go home, forget the *Sanguine Tortuga*, and abandon the fire deep in my core.

I had to. For my father and for Tristan.

CHAPTER ELEVEN

The Star on the Map

W e abandoned Mr. Hackney's crew, as well as five acquirees, on an island without a name. I had full intentions of going with them, but the night before, Theo came into my room and stopped me.

"Leena," he said from the doorway.

"Hari already tried to stop me. I can't stay aboard a ship with the...with someone who played a part in my father's death!" I spat as he entered.

"You realize she was the same age as you when your father passed," he said without flinching.

I glowered at the wall. "What does that matter?"

"It is only something to consider."

"Even if she didn't play a part in it... I can't live a life like... like this." I stared at my hands. "I'm not a murderer."

"I understand." Theo joined my side. "But I implore you to wait before you leave."

"I can't—"

"Leena…I've seen potential fates with my sight. If you leave now, I don't see you ever reuniting with your brother.

"You're just saying that to keep me here."

"How would you get home?" Theo asked. "We're depositing everyone on an island, days from the mainland. We can't guarantee anyone will find them. And even if you do, you'd have to cross the Gonvernnes continent and sail even further to get to Janis. Do you want to take that risk? All I want is for you to think… and weigh your options."

I stared at the bed, tears welling in my eye.

Theo left me without saying another word. Why didn't anyone ever finish what they wanted to say? Why was I left floundering alone on this ship, feeling like an outcast even amongst my own friends?

But perhaps Theo was right. I had no plan outside of leaving the ship. The future remained foiled with uncertainty. A decision like this required thought.

I pushed my clothes back beneath the bunk. The least I could do was wait until we returned to dry land. For now, I'd avoid June like the plague. I wouldn't be her weapon. Instead, I'd keep my fire in tow, my anger in my stomach, and my duties quiet and obedient.

But I couldn't stay hidden in my cabin forever. Hari would come pulling me out by my shirt. So after mulling about for another few minutes, I forced myself back onto the deck, choosing a corner where I could watch as the boat of Mr. Hackney's remaining crew and acquirees vanished against the thrashing waves. Now, only twelve of us remained on board: June, Hari, Pickford, Theo, Callum, Essie, Zhong, Jazmyn, Kamalani, Erik, Sloan, and me. It made me feel small on the ship. I could slip away, become no more than a mouse living in the boxes.

But fire can't hide.

My attention fell on June, as it always did. She drew me forward like a magnet, but I refused to approach her. I *would not* approach her. She danced circles on my heart, but I refused to let my mind fall into the center of the dance.

Even with her deep black hair and compelling gaze, I could not let her lure me. She was like a siren from one of Pickford's stories, nothing more. But those sirens always drew people to their deaths.

Always.

There was no way around it.

I looked away from her as the water blew off the waves, hitting me in the face. Wincing, I wiped away the water from my face. Another spout dampened my eyepatch, pressing it into the empty void in my face.

I cursed, removed it, and covered that side of my face with my hair. The mere idea of letting anyone see my scar still bothered me after all these years. I'd only shown it once to Theo, but otherwise, I kept my face hidden.

But nothing went unnoticed by June Lok.

She emerged before me like a cyclone. I couldn't even stop her as she grabbed my face. Every function in my body stopped. Would she hold me there forever, our eyes locked, our faces close? Warmth rose through my stomach as she pushed back my hair. Her attention focused solely on the scar.

"Where did you get this?"

"Wha—what?"

"The scar! How long have you had this?" She clenched my face tighter. "Tell me!"

"I got it from Venom Mouth when I was ten years old!"

June stepped back, observing me. Her voice came as a gasp. "Of course…"

I stepped back.

"Come! I need to see something!" She snagged my arm again.

I pulled away. "June, I'm not getting involved in any more of your schemes."

Her face softened. It was a rare occurrence. Usually, she held such strange determination and guile. But when I spoke those words, it was as if something had been taken from her, ripped from her throat, and unfurled on deck.

She pulled back her worries, repositioning her mask of determination before continuing, "Your face holds the clue to our treasure."

"I don't care about treasure!" I spat. "I don't work with pirates… especially the daughter of the one who killed my father!"

"What are you talking about?"

My anger continued to well in my core. "I've heard already. You're Venom Mouth's daughter. Venom Mouth killed my father and took my eye! Why would I work with *you*?"

June scoffed, "I am not Venom Mouth's daughter. That's just a story I tell."

"You're lying. You just want to use me as your weapon or something!"

"I do want you to stay, but because you are a valuable asset."

"Oh, I'm an asset now? Lovely!"

"Everyone here is an asset. You think I am on this ship for friendship?" June stepped toward me. "I am here for survival, Leena. Nothing more. Everything I do is for survival. And that is why I told the captain of the *Cobalt Hare* that I was Venom Mouth's daughter. That way, she would see me as valuable… even though I'd only been on Venom Mouth's ship for a couple years at the time. So if you think I was there when my Venom Mouth killed your daddy, well… sorry. I probably wasn't."

I didn't move, eyeing her carefully. She was merely steps from me, so close that I could feel every pulse of her breath.

"I can't trust you. I saw what you did…"

"And I've seen what you can do." June took another step forward, her face so close I could almost taste it. "Stay with me for one adventure. If you do not trust me after that, then I will help you home. Is that a deal?"

I inhaled once, taking in the scent of the sea and limiting the beats of my heart, then said, "Very well. But do not lie to me about why you want me here. You want me as a weapon for whatever adventure you wish to sail. That is all. I am nothing else to you. That much I know."

I said it more for myself than anything else.

She smiled at me, still so close that I swore I could taste her. When she spoke, her words vibrated against my skin. "That is all I ask. Now come with me."

My entire body trembled as June led me to the captain's quarters. Why did she have this hold over me? I was determined to not fall into her trap, only to be wrapped around her fingers again and dragged back through the heat of pure desire. I still didn't trust her. In fact, I was certain every word she spoke was merely a lie. But she drew me along with temptation and control, and despite the anger in my core, I agreed to follow her.

The map lay strewn across the desk, overlooking the sea, with notes scribbled in the unfamiliar language.

"Is that Yilkan?" I asked, recalling how Pickford said he couldn't translate it.

"Yilkan… yes… that's what they call it here." June huffed.

"Is that not what it's called?"

"People have changed the name of my home country and its language many times. *Yilk…* that's what they call it after years of being conquered and controlled by other nations. But I call it Sīchóu Shíyóu. We speak Sī yǔ… not *Yilkan.*"

"But everyone calls it Yilk!"

"Just because everyone calls it that, it doesn't mean that's its name." June stared at the map, tracing one of the words with her fingers.

I stared at the map. *Sīchóu Shíyóu.* It was much prettier than the name *Yilk.* I guess I never thought of how countries came to be; I always accepted my life by the sea. I never thought we came from anywhere else. But, everywhere had its own history. Just like each of us on board this ship came from different places, so did our homes.

I licked my lip, then asked, "But you can read the map? It's in...Sī yǔ?"

"Ay... I can read it. But it didn't make much sense..." she traced the border of one of the continents. Beneath it, she'd scribbled in the translation for each word. Then, her fingers rested on a giant red mark in the center of the sea. "We're here. Right here, where this mark is. But... there is no treasure. So I wasn't sure if I was reading the map wrong. That is... until I saw your eye."

"My eye?" I reached for my eyepatch, only to find it still hadn't returned to my face.

"That mark... It's Venom Mouth's signature. I didn't even notice it right down here..." June trailed her finger down the side of the map, to the smudge I'd noticed earlier. I'd assumed it was nothing more than Venom Mouth's insignia.

June fixated on it. "This is where the treasure lies."

I walked to the other side of the desk to get a better look. The scribbles of the map made my head spin, but I remained focused on the little mark identical to my scar.

"Where is that, though?" I asked.

"South. See here?" June traced along the edge of the largest continent. "This is Gonvernnes. We're going to sail down her coast, past the southern tip, and into the Burgundy Sea. There we'll find Venom Mouth's treasure."

"Are you sure?"

"I might've only been part of Venom Mouth's crew for a couple years, but I know what their signature is. Their treasure is down there... and we're gonna be the ones to find it."

"But what is their treasure?"

"That's the beauty, isn't it? No one knows. But I'm sure... we're gonna be rich. Why else would Bernard be obsessed with this map here, hm?"

I reexamined the map. Riches? Treasure? I never even thought about anything like that. But, if we found it, a realm of possibilities would lie before me. I could return home to my brother, start up a life, and never worry again!

Plus, wouldn't I get to see something far more amazing? I'd been stuck on this boat for years. Now, once at least, I could go on an adventure.

Even if it meant I had to follow a pirate into these sanguine tides.

"Fine. I'll stay for this one adventure." I whispered.

June smirked.

I immediately interjected, "Only because I am curious. Nothing more."

Of course, I was lying. I knew that. June knew that. Everyone knew that.

But I wouldn't let myself speak the truth.

CHAPTER TWELVE

On the Horizon

June told the rest of the crew about the treasure later that evening. From then on, speculation of the treasure dictated nearly every conversation. Gold? Jewels? A monster's lair? At night around the table that used to be in Mr. Hackney's private dining, we tossed around our ideas. June would sit at the helm of it all, listening with her feet up on the table, that damn smirk on her face.

I tried not to look at her. The way she held the room made me queasy. Why did she captivate me still? I didn't know.

So I kept my attention on my duties. They had changed little during the day. In fact, I'd say they had tripled. With only a fractional crew, we all had to pick up the slack to keep the ship working. Theo almost never left the crow's nest, while Hari maintained inventory and kept the crew at ease. Pickford spent a lot of time with Erik, our new chef, in the galley, sorting through his hidden stash of food. Then there was Callum, who spent most of his time following Hari around like a lost puppy. She didn't mind, though. It was sweet; they spoke together with their heads close, shoulders closer. Some days, I'd catch them holding hands. Without Mr. Hackney to watch over them, Callum seemed a tad less stingy. He no longer greased back his blond hair, and every once in a while, I swore he smiled.

But despite everyone finding their rhythm, I did the same work as before with no change: clean the decks, secure the belongings, and run errands.

I swore, no matter where I was, June watched.

In my cabin, I found solace. With only twelve people on board, we each received our own cabins. I relocated to one on the lower deck, with a port side window where I stared out at sea. There, no one bothered me, and I had time to collect my thoughts and practice my flame.

Whenever I practiced, I did nothing too outlandish. Rather, I cupped small flickers of fire in my hands and let them hover over my palms, all before diminishing into the darkness. I still didn't understand the magic. If I closed my eye, I could almost see a different life: one where my father taught Tristan and me about our powers and where we mastered the fire together as one, with our futures paved in certainty.

My heart ached thinking of Tristan. I hadn't written to him in years. What did he think happened to me?

What had happened to him?

Was he taking care of our mother? Did he join the navy like our father? Was he happy?

These thoughts stayed with me as we ate around the table every night, only to be interrupted by the lavish tales and speculation about the treasure.

"It's probably gold," Callum said as he picked at his food one evening.

"C'mon, Cal," Pickford said with a mouthful of food, "you're an artist! You gotta be more creative than that!"

"But that's what pirates want. Gold and jewels."

"You're no fun!"

"I—"

Hari came to Callum's rescue. "Even if it is gold and jewels, imagine what that might do for all of us. We'd be able to do anything."

"Yeah, but it could be so much more amazing!"

"Oh, you mean like your siren stories?"

"The treasure could be sirens, for all you know!"

Theo interjected, "I've told you before... sirens don't exist. It's just a story."

"Then nymphs... or dryads! Perhaps a vampire!"

"They don't exist either."

"Bah, shush. Let a man dream. What do you think it is? Or have you already seen and won't say?"

"I haven't seen anything about the treasure. But it isn't sirens."

Pickford threw his arms back in defeat. "Why is everyone so uncreative?"

Hari turned to me. "Leena! You've been so quiet! What do you think it is?"

I raised my head. From the corner of my eye, I noticed June shift in her seat slightly. I picked up my jug of water and took a sip, then stared hard at the liquid. What did I consider treasure? Growing up, gold wasn't considered a treasure. There was something else far more important and far more expensive.

"Fresh water," I said.

"Water?" Pickford scoffed in disgust.

"Back on my home island of Janis, we valued fresh water. There weren't many sources on the island, and if you didn't pay your taxes, then you had no water. We valued it more than anything. So maybe... it's a lagoon of fresh water we can barrel up and sell to islands like my home."

Pickford grunted, "I'm gonna stick with my siren story."

Hari rolled her eyes, then continued down the table for other opinions. Kamalani mentioned magic crystals, while Jazmyn toyed with the idea of sea monsters. The stories circulated about the table as everyone joked and laughed. All the while, I shrank back into my chair, blood rushing to my cheeks. Why would I say water? What sort of answer was that?

Yet, June didn't show any sort of interest in other stories. After I finished my thought, I noticed as she sank back into the chair and continued to pick at her fingers.

I didn't look up from my food for the rest of the evening.

Once I finished, I left the table in a hurry. Again, nausea had become my friend, and I vomited over the side of the ship. June had this way of seeping into me, and I failed to shake it. Could she read my thoughts? Was she invading mine? Did she use magic to manipulate me? Or was it just my paranoia?

So I reminded myself, just one adventure. One more adventure.

"You alright there?"

I jumped. Of course June approached! Why wouldn't she? With that calm swagger in her walk and a smirk on her lips, she joined me at the railing and glanced down the hull.

"You vomit?" she asked.

"Everyone vomits," I grumbled.

"I mean, right now, did you vomit?"

"Yeah, sorry... my stomach hurt." I didn't look at her, keeping my eye on the horizon. The hair on my arm rose as she leaned over the edge of the ship to peer down the side.

"That's impressive. It's all the way down the side." She laughed a strange warm laugh I didn't think she'd ever produce. "There is clearly something else going on with you."

"There's nothing wrong with me!" I snapped.

She smirked and leaned back on her heels. "Do I fluster you, Leena?"

"Of course you fluster me! You're a pirate and—"

"Not like that." She gripped the railing, still smiling in my direction. "I meant at a more personal level."

I turned away. She laughed again.

We didn't speak after that for a few minutes. I hoped she would walk away, but she stayed with her attention locked on the sea.

Her tune changed when she spoke again. "Fresh water? Is that really considered treasure to you?"

"Yes, for a lot of the islanders…" I adjusted my eyepatch. "On Janis, we had one freshwater spring owned by the governor. We ventured once a week to fill up barrels, but if the spring ran dry, then those of us on the far end of the island were out of luck. So we would barter with ships like this to get water. But it's not like we had money or anything."

I licked my bottom lip. There had been countless days when my mother, brother, and I had to share a single canteen of water. Sometimes, I went to the sea and drank salt water, only to have to use our small outhouse for hours that evening. But when you were desperate, you drank what you found.

"Hm." June said nothing else, once again enthralled with the sea. I didn't expect her to say anything. Why would she? It probably sounded ridiculous.

In fact, it sounded ridiculous. Who would want to find *water* as a treasure?

June wanted something spectacular. She yearned for something that would change her life. Not some water.

But she didn't show any disappointment, her attention attached to the sea. "Do you see that?"

"See what?" I followed her gaze but saw nothing. "I'm half-blind. Can't see anything."

"There's a ship out there." She smirked at me. "We can take it, I bet."

"What? Why!?"

"The more the merrier, hm? Plus, we need more supplies before we reach the treasure."

"June—"

Before I objected, she raced to the bell on deck and rang it. It echoed across the deck, and one at a time, each crew member emerged from different spots on the ship.

Pickford rubbed his eyes, squinting, while Theo descended from his spot in the crow's nest. I didn't even know he was up there! Did he hear everything June said to me?

I truly hoped his hearing wasn't as good as his sight.

"What's going on?" Hari asked, her hand wrapped around Callum's wrist as she emerged from below deck.

June hopped on a crate. "There's a ship! Pretty sure it's part of the *Commeant*. I think we can take it. Bring aboard more acquirees, really form this crew! We can show those slavers yet that they do not rule the seas—"

"That's ridiculous," Callum interjected at once.

"Pardon?" June stared at him. Callum hadn't said much of anything since Mr. Hackney died, but this time, he spoke without hesitation.

"We hardly have a crew. That ship could be bigger than us! Or with more skilled fighters. It doesn't make sense to fight—"

"And why should I listen to you?" June hissed. "What do you know of the sea? The only reason I kept you on board is because Hari vouched for you."

"I'm just thinking logically—"

"And I think you're—"

Theo interjected, "I have to agree with Callum. I saw the ship, and it is at least double our size. We don't have the power to take it. Not yet at least."

"We have a pyromancer!" June waved her hands in front of me. That was really why June was fascinated by me. I had to remind myself of that. I was nothing more than her little weapon.

Hari spoke next: "With all respect to Leena…she only just discovered her magic. She needs time to learn how to control it. It's too soon, June."

June scowled. "Does anyone else not want to attack this ship?"

Everyone raised their hand.

Except me.

I instead bled into the darkness of the night, taking one step back at a time to escape June's discontent.

This was not my battle to fight.

After all, I promised one adventure.

Just one.

CHAPTER THIRTEEN

São Caméliosa

June didn't venture from her cabin for three days. I took it as a saving grace. Really, I didn't need her loitering about, drawing my attention away from my duties. Ever since no one agreed with her plan to siege the ship, she became a recluse. Everyone spoke from their heart that night. Going after the ship would have been futile; we were a broken crew of pirates.

Pirates...

The mere word caused my stomach to turn.

My father would roll in his grave if he knew what became of me. A pirate!

No. This was one adventure. One chance at freedom. Then I was done with June Lok and her antics.

But after three days, as the ship voyaged to São Camé-liosa's port, June ventured onto the deck. I didn't move from my spot by the bow, keeping my eye lowered. She reached the edge of the deck, watching as the coastline came into view, hair whipping over her face.

"We'll be in port in about an hour!" Theo called from the crow's nest.

June said nothing. For a moment, she remained there before returning to her cabin with a scowl on her face.

"She's an odd one, ain't she?" Pickford asked me from his spot on the crates.

"Huh?" I glanced at him.

"June. She's an odd one. Great pirate, but there's a lot going on in that head of hers... kind of ridiculous, if you ask me."

"I don't think she lived a great life," I mumbled.

"So you're getting acquainted with the pirate, hm?"

"I don't want to! She keeps talking to me."

"Mhm..." Pickford smirked.

"What?"

"You're turning red."

"I am not!" But I felt my cheeks warm at the mere mention of June.

"Admit you're at least a little fascinated by her. Even I'm a little interested, and she's not really my type." Pickford brushed his locks back behind his ear dramatically. "June Lok, the mysterious and murderous pirate, with her beautiful hair and unusual waltz." He hopped on another crate and stood with his hands on his hips. "June Lok, queen of the seas, who freed us with her guile and pride. Oh, and have you seen June Lok, with her strong shoulders, her chiseled jaw, and her—"

"Enough!" I covered my ears, "Stop!"

"Just admit it. Your secret is safe with me."

"No, it isn't! You told everyone the moment Hari and Callum went into the crow's nest!"

Pickford chuckled, "Fine. But I still know you *like* her."

I stuck my tongue out at him, then stomped across the deck to finish mopping the farthest corner away from Pickford.

We docked in São Caméliosa around midday. No one questioned a cohort of washed-up sailors on an obsidian ship, and they welcomed us without issue. Other than Theo, everyone eagerly hurried to the gangway. My stomach bounced; I hadn't been off the ship in years! Would I even remember how to walk?

I waited in the back of the line as everyone exited the ship. Hari and Callum rushed off, hand-in-hand, whispering with their heads close. Ever since Mr. Hackney fell to his death, they'd been inseparable. They shared a cabin, sat next to each other during meals, and even kissed on deck without fear. Hari's smile had become her trademark, stifling the sadness that hid in her eyes for years. Callum remained his quiet, frail self, but he at least had a voice. He followed Hari around like he did with Mr. Hackney, but at least here, they saw each other as equals.

Pickford ventured off as soon as he arrived in the gangway with Erik and Kamalani into the droves of merchants. He mentioned something about acquiring more chocolate and other wares for the kitchen, but before I asked to join, he long abandoned me.

The excitement was contagious. For the first time, we could explore without Mr. Hackney! We were free!

But I hesitated to step off the gangway.

"You going ashore?"

I hadn't heard June come up beside me. I nearly jumped when I saw her. Instead of her typical loose blouse, corset, pants, and boots, she wore a large hoop skirt with a flowing petticoat. She had pinned her hair up on her head. She even wore lip paint and blush!

I stammered, "Are you going somewhere?"

"Oh, this? I don't want to be recognized here."

"You've been here before?"

"A few years ago, Venom Mouth docked here and caused a scuffle. Got a little involved." June shrugged. "Honestly, if you don't want to leave the ship, there ain't much in São Caméliosa. Really just a place for gardeners and merchants and such."

"I do want to get off! I haven't been off in years!"

"Then what're you waiting for?"

"Nothing! See!" I stepped ashore. The moment I hit the ground, vertigo took over, and my entire body rocked. Vomit rose in my throat, then fell again, and I inhaled once more to regain my balance. The ground moved as I stepped forward, and I swore I would fall over on my side.

"You got to get your land legs back," June said as she jumped onto land. Her cocky smile lit up her face.

But as soon as she landed, she nearly fell.

I rushed over to her. Why did I? It seemed to come naturally as she stumbled.

The captain took my arm, and after a moment, she regained her footing.

"Guess you don't have your land legs either." I chided.

She huffed.

For a moment, we stood there. She continued gripping my arm. For the first time, she lost that strange confidence and allure. June Lok became merely a young woman, lost and unsure, as the ground rocked beneath us.

As if she realized my thoughts, she pulled away and straightened her back. "Well... I got things to do."

"Like what?"

"Pirate shit."

"Aren't we just in port to—ugh!" She walked away before I finished my sentence. Despite the wobbling of my feet, I rushed behind her, following her out of port and into town. People bustled through the town area. Ivy covered the buildings, pulling the manmade structures back into nature with a single gasp of green and a flush of multi-colored flowers. The people even belonged in nature, with flowers in their hair, vines laced along their skin, and roots clawing at their feet.

I joined June's side, trying not to stare at these nature-based people. "Are these dryads or nymphs or something? Like what Pickford talks about?"

"Nah. They're just a bunch of gardeners." June said without looking at me.

"Just gardeners? Not all gardeners become part plant!"

June rolled her eyes. "Fine. *Magic* gardeners."

I stared in awe as I walked past another group of individuals with crowns of flowers on their heads.

In all honesty, the town of São Caméliosa had more green than I ever saw. Back in Janis, the world pulsed with brown. At sea, while the water shimmered beneath the blue sky, spots of darkness waited to inhale the ships. The clouds bled with dust.

But São Caméliosa bled green.

How could June say there wasn't anything special about this place?

June didn't stop to dawdle. I didn't have to follow her. As much as I wanted to keep staring at this beautiful town, my feet carried me behind her like a loyal pet.

I rubbed my hands together. Heat thumped between my palms, threatening to catch fire. I swallowed it back and jammed my hands in my pockets. Did these gardeners' magic behave just like my fire? Did it come from their soul and emotions, just like my flame?

June led me out of town, over the cracked cobblestone roads, and deep into the trees. Despite the roots and branches tearing at her dress, she didn't flinch. Her attention latched forward on some invisible goal.

I kept quiet. Every few steps, I paused and considered turning around but kept following her. Besides, if she got in trouble... who would help? We would wait on our boat for her return, only to be left without a captain.

Sure, Hari might take control of the ship, but something about June made the *Sanguine Tortuga* feel... powerful.

The trees thinned as we reached the end of the road. There, a wrought-iron gate waited. A plaque sat on it, with a single message engraved:

Propriedad d'los Gardeniros n'e Diversito

"What's that mean?" I asked as June pushed open the gate.

"Something about gardeners. I don't speak Vernnes."

"Oh. I just thought since you speak Yil—I mean Sī yǔ that you might—"

"Completely different languages. Ask Pickford to translate it." June passed through the gate, creeping along the broken path. Flowers filled the bushes before us, like a rainbow of color, with petals catching wind and flying into the sky. One caught June's hair, like a single white ship resting on a sea of silky black. I almost reached forward to remove it but caught my hand.

"Why are we here?" I asked June.

"What does it matter? You didn't have to come."

"I…" Why did I come? I tried to avoid June almost every day. Why today? I concocted a reason. "I didn't have anywhere else to go."

It wasn't a lie, either.

June shrugged. "Well, we're not anywhere special. These are the governor's gardens."

"And?"

"And what?"

"You're here for a reason."

June groaned. "Just know that if this goes according to plan, we'll be rich."

"What are you talking about?"

"Nothing. Just keep an eye out for soldiers. And stop asking questions."

"Soldiers!?" I half-laughed. "We're doing something illegal?"

"I never asked you to follow me."

"Yeah, but this is a quick stop—"

"I'm a pirate. I'll do what I need to do." June waved her hand. "Just watch for soldiers or whatever. Or leave. Whatever makes the most sense. Doubt there'll be any... they're probably all off fighting in their civil war."

"Civil war?"

"You don't know anything, do you?"

"I was stuck on a ship for years. Not the best place to get an education. And it's not like I got the most relevant news growing up in Janis either."

"I see."

"So, can you please tell me?"

"Fine," June replied, "Gonvernnes has been stuck in a civil war for years. Something to do with trade relations and magic and such. Don't ask me the details—not my forte. None of it matters. We got our own nation to lead aboard the Tortuga."

"Oh, okay..." I glanced over my shoulder, then spun around to check my sides. Hadn't people learned by now that I wasn't really a good watchguard? I only had one eye!

June marched ahead undisturbed. The swagger had returned to her walk. As she walked, she plucked leaves from the evenly trimmed hedges. The roots failed to trip her, and each step forward came with the determination of a queen. What was she looking for in this garden? What could be so important that she risked being caught *by soldiers*? Maybe this could count for my adventure, and rather than boarding the *Sanguine Tortuga* again, I could wait for another ship to come and take me home.

Yet I knew June would not accept that option.

We passed under an archway that led us into a weaving pathway through bushes covered in white flowers. A few soldiers waited, but none stopped us, a performative measure to watch over the enchanted garden. As we walked, the flowers shimmered as if covered in a permanent layer of dew. In certain lights, they reflected the color of the sky, of the leaves, and of June's mahogany dress.

Like magic.

June ran her finger along a flower's petal. "We're close…"

"What are these?"

"Some flower that has to do with the magic here or something. I don't know. Not worth much to me." She crushed the flower petal between her fingers. "Come along now."

I glanced behind us, then followed June deeper into the gardens. To my relief, no one loitered in the gardens. June almost looked like she belonged in her long mahogany dress and combed hair. If I didn't know, I would never have thought she was a pirate.

Past the droves of white flowered bushes, a clearing of pristine green grass beneath the watch of a palace waited for us.

June did not approach the palace, her path directed toward the courtyard lined with hedges instead. Once again, I checked for any soldiers, but the garden seemed otherwise silent.

"If luck is on our side, the governor isn't home. Perhaps they fled the oncoming storm of war," June said as she tiptoed through the courtyard.

"Can you tell me what we're here for now?"

"Impatient, aren't you?"

"I've been following you for the past hour."

"I didn't ask you to follow."

"Yes, but—"

"But what?"

I flushed but swallowed down my nerves. "As a member of your crew, it is my prerogative to make sure you do not get harmed."

"Mhm." June smirked and turned down another path.

I would have replied, but my mouth fell open around the bend, and every objection I had vanished.

There, contained by a cage of thorns and vines, sat a single flower on a pedestal. At first glance, it looked like nothing more than the white flowers on the nearby pushes. But as June and I approached, it became clear that it was so much more.

"Excellent..." June whispered, taking a step toward the thorn cage and unfurling her dagger from the inside of her coat. As she reached for them, the thorned branches thickened, guarding the flower with the sharp-toothed nature of a wild beast.

"What's so important about that flower?"

"It's the pearl camellia," June said, glancing at me.

"The pearl camellia?"

"This flower has existed for centuries, rumored to be born from pearls itself, and more valuable than a pound of gold. Venom Mouth tried grabbing this gem years ago. Didn't quite work out."

"And you want to steal it now?" I asked.

"One petal could help us barter for the unthinkable." June paced around the thorn-riddled cage. "Imagine what we might accomplish."

I stared at the flower. Its petals shimmered in my direction, like the pearls my mother used to own.

June circled the cage. "Last time, this wasn't so guarded. Guess they learned better."

"You were there when Venom Mouth tried stealing it?"

"Yeah. Was part of my first heist. Hence the disguise." She curtsied dramatically in her oversized dress.

If I hadn't seen her on the ship, I might not have recognized her in a crowd.

"Let's get this beauty out of here now." June placed her dagger to the wall of thorns and sawed open their grasp. Carefully, she reached through the opening.

But the thorns acted with vengeance. Despite her dexterity, they still reached out and pricked her fingers in a single breath.

June stepped back and stared at the blood on her finger. Her eyes widened, and she stumbled back, nearly collapsing into my arms.

"June!" I grabbed her arm to keep her from falling to the ground.

She swayed to the side.

"June! What is it? What's wrong?"

"Poison on the thorn..." she hissed. The fingers of her left hand turned black in a matter of seconds, the poison already beginning its climb up her hand.

I snatched her hand, staring at the wound. "We need to get you back to the ship... or ask for help... or... or something!"

"I'm fine. Really. We came this far..." she simpered. Her cheeks lost color, eyes already growing distant.

"But it's going—"

"We came for the flower. We'll get the flower and worry about my hand later." She fell to her knees, eyes still laced on the pearl camellia.

What could I do? In some ways, I was responsible for the captain. I traveled with her as her crewmate. But I was no medic. How could I neutralize the poison or rid it of her blood?

My stomach flipped as an idea came to mind.

Trembling, I took her hand and raised it to my lips. My mouth trembled as I placed my lips on the cut. I sucked on the wound, praying to whatever god might listen that I managed to remove the poison.

Would this even work? It seemed like a myth or a story that Pickford once told. A kiss to remove poison? I had my doubts.

But I had to try.

Her skin felt rough on my lips, worn by years at sea. Yet, she tasted like the ocean. I held my lips there, and after sucking the blood away from the small cut, I spat on the ground to avoid the poison's rage.

"I told you, I'm okay…" June whispered and pressed her fingers to my chin, holding me there for a minute. Her eyes still hung heavy with pain. A smirk crossed her face.

"You know, sucking out poison like that doesn't really work," she said.

"I—" My face warmed.

"But I guess it neutralized it for now. It's still there, but it's not moving quickly. The magic of a kiss, hm?" She leaned forward, her lips close, her breath hitting my skin. Part of me leaned forward, begging for her taste, but I stepped back. No. She was dangerous. I could not fall for her toxic allure.

A smile stuck on her face. She stepped away from me. Her attention fell back to the flower. It remained clear on her face how much the poison continued to impact her. She swayed back and forth on her feet. Would I have to bring her hand to my mouth again?

"Let's get that flower and get out of here," she muttered.

"Shouldn't we head back to town to get an antidote?"

"I'm fine for now. Stop worrying."

"But how do we get the flower out without hurting ourselves more?"

"Simple. You."

"What?"

"I'm lucky my little pyromancer followed me." June stepped back. "Go on."

Part of me wanted to argue, but as always, June pulled the strings. The heat had made its way into my palms. Those thorns had injured my captain, and I would make them pay.

The fire gathered in my hand, and without touching the thorns, I guided the flame onto the cage around the pearl. Sizzling, the flame moved down the stem, eating away at the thorns and casting them to the ground like molted skin.

June didn't wait until the fire stopped to grab the pearl camellia. In an instant, it vanished from its pedestal and disappeared into her pocket.

"C'mon. Let's get outta here." She motioned me to follow.

"What about the fire? And your hand?"

"It'll burn out. C'mon!"

She snagged my arm with her good hand, dragging me away from the courtyard. Our footsteps echoed as we ran.

Soon, they multiplied. Not only did our footsteps echo, but others in the distance.

One... two...

One... two...

One...

"Halt!" someone shouted. "What're you doing here?"

I turned to see a cohort of soldiers running down the path, swords extended and ready to attack. With everything that happened, I'd lost track of the soldiers. I froze. What could I do? I was supposed to be watching them—even though they had seemed quite disengaged. I guess my flame was enough of a beacon to summon them.

But June did not hesitate to fight. She instantly grabbed my hand and held it out. Her lips fell close to my ear.

"Burn them all," she whispered, her lips brushing against my skin.

My insides twisted. Heat rose from my core and through my skin.

And with a single breath, fire exploded from my palm, engulfing the slew of oncoming soldiers and the surrounding garden.

CHAPTER FOURTEEN

Cauterized

Even from the ship, I could see the flames rising over the port, engulfing the magic that defined its beauty. My heart broke for it; I didn't mean to cause such destruction. But June and I had to get out of there; I'd only just claimed my freedom. I couldn't have it stolen from me again.

My hands continued to pulse with fire. Once back on board the *Sanguine Tortuga*, I found a bucket of water and kept it close. Every time even a flicker of flame willed itself into my palms, I dunked my hands in the water to stop it from taking shape.

June and I told no one what happened. Once the rest of the crew returned to the boat, whispers traveled about an attack from the Eastern Coast, part of their ongoing civil war. The only one who probably knew the truth was Theo, who watched closely as I moved about the deck. June vanished almost immediately upon arrival to fawn over her new gem.

As we sailed off into the sunset, the ship returned to its quiet rhythm. I found a crate to sit upon and watch as São Caméliosa disappeared into the horizon, mangled by a cloud of smoke.

I felt worse about the gardens succumbing to my flame than the soldiers I harmed. If they survived, they would have a nice souvenir. But those gardens, the magic they held, I had destroyed it all with a single wave of my hand. Would it be like that forever? Would they regrow?

Or would they sit there, nothing more than weeds, burnt away by the clumsy hand of a pirate?

Pirate.

That word haunted my every thought.

I didn't hear as Theo, Pickford, Callum, and Hari approached me that evening. My eye remained locked on the horizon.

"Leena, eat." Hari handed me a bowl of fruit.

"Not hungry." I glanced at the fruit. The colors were far too bright for today.

"Fine, I'll eat it!" Pickford reached for my bowl of fruit, but Hari smacked his hand away. He brought it to his mouth and kissed it.

"You haven't left this spot in three hours. Are you okay?" Hari pressured, sitting down on the crate next to me.

"Yeah, I'm fine."

Hari gave that look where I knew she wouldn't drop the conversation.

I sighed, weaving a lie around my truth. "With the garden burning... and all this talk of the Eastern side attacking... I guess I'm concerned about the war in Gonvernnes. I didn't even know about it. Having been on this ship... I lost a chance at a formal education or anything like that."

"That war's been going on forever," Pickford said as he snagged a piece of coconut from the fruit bowl.

"Yes, but why? What if it impacts us somehow?"

"I don't see it affecting us," Theo said.

"But we have magic!" The lie started to get to me, filling my chest with anxiety. There was far too much to worry about here. "June said it had to do with magic or something. I don't know. There's so much I don't know."

To my surprise, Callum spoke next, almost in a whisper, "You don't need to worry about your magic in Gonvernnes. Most magic there is plant-based, held close by the Gardeniros. The concern over magic, and the war that was built around it, argues that the Gardeniros interfere with the natural order of the world. They keep the world green, but some believe the world needs to go through its changes to thrive. They don't care about your fire or Theo's sight. It's not a native part of this region."

I stared at Callum.

And Pickford spoke my thoughts. "You know about that shit?"

"I…like history. My father made sure I learned. Said it was important if I ever… well… yeah." He looked at his hands.

Before Pickford could grill him more, I interjected, "Wait! You said my magic isn't native to this region! Where does it come from then? The islands?"

"No…no. There's been a lot of immigration and such between the Western and Eastern Continents. Here, we can look at a map, and I'll show you. I think it's fascinating, honestly."

I glanced at Hari, and with a nod, I hopped off the crate to follow Callum. Never did it occur to me that Callum had this knowledge. While Theo had a general knowledge and could see so much about the present, when I asked about his magic, he would just shrug.

Ever since June came into power, the doors to the bridge of the ship remained open. We passed Essie as we ventured inside, a compass and spyglass in hand as she walked toward the helm on deck. She didn't say a word to us, leaving Callum and me in the private company of a map on the table.

I stared at the map, focused entirely on the southeastern continent and the varying seas. It lacked the complexity or artistry of the treasure map, far more lucid in its presentation. Callum pointed to the southwest edge of the Eastern Continent. "This is where we are now, off the coast of Gonvernnes."

I followed his fingers, staring at the intricacies of the coastlines. "Where's Janis?"

He traced his fingers along the southern tip of the continent, then to a small island on the eastern side. "Right here. We circumnavigated the southern tip over a year ago."

"I'm that far from home!?" Queasiness returned at the realization. We traveled so far! How would I ever get home?

"We cover a lot of the sea. After picking you up in Janis, we headed to San Joya right here." He indicated a spot on the eastern side of the continent. "Then we circumnavigated the continent. We met up with the *Cobalt Hare* up here, in the northwestern corner." He tapped another spot on the map. "And now we're heading south again, probably somewhere past Jrin Ayl." He pointed to a large island off the southern edge of the continent.

"That's where Hari is from, right?"

"Mhm." Callum blinked a couple times. "They say the magic of Jrin Ayl focuses on internal balance, aim, etcetera. Think of Hari's perfect aim. Might be because of talent, but there's definitely a magical element."

I said nothing, taking in each of Callum's words.

When I didn't speak, Callum continued. "On the Western Continent, we have Yilk—"

"Sīchóu Shíyóu," I corrected him.

"Right. Sīchóu Shíyóu." He licked his lip, then continued. "There is evidence of giants and other magic there. Just north of it, you have Delilah." He motioned to another nation. "There's no true natural magic in Delilah. It's a hodgepodge. Some say they were once part of Yilk—I mean, Sīchóu Shíyóu—but ultimately divided themselves because of cultural differences."

"Are they the ones who call it Yilk?"

"Possibly. The cultures of the two sides were very different. It's possible that a lot of those in Delilah came from the northern Spinozan region, too."

"Spinoza…" I recited.

"That is one of interest to you. It is the land of fire and dragons."

"Dragons are myths."

"So some say." He kept his finger on that northern region. "Either way, you probably have heritage from that region that allows you to control fire."

"But what am I doing here?"

"Immigration. Colonialization. Conquerors. People have moved around the world. There is no one region anymore. The *Commeant* carries some of the responsibility as well."

"That's what we were part of, right?"

"Yes. They take people from all corners of the world... just like Mr. Hackney has done with all of us." Callum paused for a second, tracing the map with his eyes.

"What about the rest of the map?" I asked. It truly fascinated me. I never thought much about the layout of our world, but so much depended on just a few little things.

"Yes, so, from Spinoza, we have the Ainan region..." Callum's fingers danced across the sea again. "We have Evylain, the Schanifeld, and Kainan. Their magic is a bit of a mystery... hardly touched at all in most studies. There are hints of a few parts of magic, but nothing clear." His fingers raced to a small nation beneath what he called the Schanifeld. "But we have Merton here. It's a small nation. Just one city, really. Seers come from there... like Theo."

"Theo said he was from Delilah, though!"

"Again, hodgepodge," Callum said, still fixated on the map as he trailed his finger from Merton, across the nation of Kainan, and back down the Eastern Continent. All of this was overwhelming, but I took each new fact in awe.

"Moving south, there's the Rosadian region. This is the land of mist and smoke." He continued along until he reached Gonvernnes and tapped the map, "And then we're back here, in the land of earth and nature... Gonvernnes." Callum grinned at me. "That's not all of it, of course.

There's so many more nations and nuance to magic, but that's the general understanding of all of this."

I took in each region of the map, trying my best to commit each magical element to memory. In the course of just a few minutes, it was like I had unlocked an entire world before me. My magic came from somewhere deep in my blood. When did my family leave Spinoza? How did they end up on Janis? The history would remain a mystery, but at least I had some answers.

"Thank you for sharing this with me, Callum. How did you learn all of this?" I asked.

"Well, I had to. My parents wanted me to—"

"Because he's Bernard Hackney's son," June's voice sliced into our conversation.

Callum and I turned at the same time. In her usual fashion, June leaned against the wall, arms crossed. Black-laced veins covered her poisoned hand.

Callum began, "How did you—"

"You have the same eyes and chin as Bernard. And it was easy to tell with how you followed him around like a lost puppy."

I turned my attention back to Callum. "You're Mr. Hackney's son? Does Hari know!?"

Callum nodded, eyes falling to the floor.

I stepped back, "But...why are you still aboard? We... I... June killed Mr. Hackney!"

"I only ever joined this ship because my mother died. I had a choice... be an orphan or join my father. He didn't even like me... thought I was useless." Callum kept his head bowed and eyes downcast. "I did all I could to impress him. Learned these here maps, learned the history, but I didn't have *talent*. Not like Hari or Pickford or Theo. He didn't value painting or anything... so I was just an annoyance."

It all made sense. No wonder he always followed behind Mr. Hackney or why he always looked so pristine. To an extent, Mr. Hackney recognized his son to avoid embarrassment. But really, he had been nothing more than an object.

"But aren't you angry?" June stepped toward Callum. "Are you not upset? Come now, I killed your father. Don't you want to seek revenge?"

"I..."

June removed a clever knife from her belt and handed it to Callum. "Go on. Seek your revenge."

He didn't take the knife.

"Here, I'll even make a suggestion," June slammed her poisoned hand on the table, "cut off my hand for me. That way, we both win. You get a taste of blood, and I get rid of this hand."

Callum took the knife and stared at its blade. For a moment, no one breathed.

Then he raised the knife...

... and stabbed the table next to June's hand.

"I'm not my father. If you really need to cut off that hand, do it yourself."

Callum left the room without waiting for June's response, slamming the door on his way out of the room.

June pulled the knife from the table with a grunt. She tapped the fingers of her injured hand on the wood. "Gotta do something about this thing. Your little kiss stopped the poison from traveling, but it's already woven its way through my hand. Don't have much feeling left in any of these here fingers anymore."

"I'm sure we can find in a doctor in the next port—"

"Next port won't be for a while."

"What about in the medic kit?"

"Already checked all the medical supplies we have onboard. No good, really." She held the knife out to me. "Chop it off."

"What!?"

"Callum didn't do it, so now I'm asking you. Chop off my hand."

"I'm not chopping off your hand!"

"You've expressed your distaste for me. Chop it off!"

"No!"

June stared at the cleaver, then shrugged.

In a single movement, she raised the blade into the air and slammed it down into her wrist.

Blood splattered.

June yelped.

And I screamed.

As blood gushed from her wound, June stumbled back, hitting the bookcase with the back of her head. On the ground, her dismembered hand twitched in a pool of red. Color left June's face as she sank to her knees.

"Leena...the wound. Cauterize the wound!" She stammered.

"Ri-right!" I raced to her side and took her handless wrist. Heat rose in my hands, and I focused only on June's face as I willed the fire into existence. Her eyes flickered between consciousness and sleep.

Despite my nerves trembling, I ordered the fire across her wound, letting the skin mold together, slowing the blood's expedition. And with it, June's breathing slowed. Her sweat-matted head fell against my shoulder with a sigh.

"What's wrong with you?!" I half laughed and half cried as we sat in the pool of blood.

"A lot of things," June mumbled as she closed her eyes, "At least I got a good first mate."

I opened my mouth, unsure how to respond. But before I could think of anything, June's breathing slowed in a rhythmic sleep, leaving me to explain what happened as Hari, Theo, and Pickford came rushing into the cabin.

CHAPTER FIFTEEN

A Phantom Hand

For almost a week, June slept. Our newly assigned medic, Zhong, stitched up June's wound and provided a slew of medications to ward off infections he had acquired in São Caméliosa. All the while, the *Sanguine Tortuga* kept on its track toward the location on the treasure map under Theo and Essie's supervision.

Despite her absence, June's presence remained, especially for me. After she cut off her hand for nearly three hours, Hari hounded me for answers about what happened. How did June get poisoned? Why didn't I stop her from cutting off her hand? Then I received a lecture about how fortunate June was that we had antiseptics and other medical supplies on board. Without them, she might have *died*.

My sole duty became tending to June as she recovered. I brought her food and water, cleaned her wounds, and kept watch. I felt obligated to help her. While none of this was my fault, I had been there through every drop of poison, every squirt of blood, and every flickering flame.

It was supposed to be one adventure, but already I wondered... would I ever be able to leave her side after this? Or was this her game, wrapping me around her finger and pulling me in tight to make me think I was valuable and deserving of her attention?

One adventure. I would remain on board for one adventure.

I was nothing more than a tool for her.

Or perhaps that was what I wanted to believe.

I kept reciting that fallacy over and over to myself as I sat beside June's bed. As I removed the bandages from her wrist, she stirred.

"Captain!" I stopped, meeting her gaze.

She glanced at me with her dark eyes half open as she smiled. Without a word, she raised her good hand to my lip and traced it with her index finger.

The world froze as she held me there, capturing me in her gaze and locking me tight with her smile. Another gasp of warmth ate inside me. What made me want her like this? She was a pirate, a member of the crew that killed my father, but in the past couple of weeks, she'd become some sort of friend.

June chuckled, "You're as red as a tomato."

"I—"

My breath escaped me as she drew me forward, her fingers delicate on my face, dancing over each of my freckles. Her lips hovered just over mine. If I moved less than an inch, I'd be able to kiss her. Would she taste like the sea? Or like chocolate and gold?

"Thank you for staying by my side through this, Leena. I appreciate it." She released me. I stumbled back, my heart clawing at my throat as I stared at her. June continued. "You can leave now. I'm okay now."

"Are—are you sure? I can—"

"Yes. Leave. Now."

"O—okay." I stepped back, staring at June one last time. She didn't call me back over to her, instead turning on her side to stare at the wall. With that, I took it as my sign to leave. So I tiptoed from her room and shut the door behind me.

That way, she didn't hear me as I sobbed.

For the first time in weeks, I joined Theo in the crow's nest, watching the sunset over the calm purple waters. As June had indicated, we began voyaging deep into the Burgundy Sea, and with each day, its name became more apparent. Some days, it reminded me of wine sifting in a glass. In another light, it permanently held the glow of dawn.

As Theo and I watched the water, we popped open a bottle of rum and shared glasses, rarely speaking. Theo kept his eyes fixated on the horizon while I reveled in the silence. It reminded me of a simpler time. Not that life aboard the *Sanguine Tortuga* had ever been simple, but more...a time when I didn't get flustered over some captain's flirtatious advances.

Well, was it flirting? Or was that just June being... June?

I glanced over the edge of the crow's nest. Hari and Callum sat in their usual corner, sharing food, heads pressed together and laughing. They seemed so natural; Hari led the relationship with her determination and pride, while Callum followed, whispering kindnesses in Hari's ears. How did they realize that they'd fallen in love? How did they know the other cared?

But they weren't June Lok. June acted of her own accord.

I had to remind myself of that. She manipulated, she controlled, and she killed.

I was a pawn in her game.

That was it.

I tried to distract myself, focusing instead on Callum. Since June cut off her hand, I had spent little time thinking about what Callum said. Nor had I really taken a moment to let the revelation sink in: Callum was Mr. Hackney's son.

Did anyone else know other than Hari, June, and me? Did Theo?

I glanced over my shoulder at Theo. He leaned against the edge, clutching the bottle of rum, his attention pulled onto the distant coastline.

"Callum taught me about where our magic came from... at least according to history," I said.

Theo nodded. "Yeah, he knows all of that stuff. It doesn't really matter anymore, though. The world has changed; we're not partitioned into factions anymore. We're just people trying to survive."

"But isn't it important to learn where we came from?"

"Eh. It can help, but it's an old way of thinking. Mr. Hackney and others like him try to compartmentalize where everyone comes from, but it doesn't work like that anymore. It doesn't surprise me that Callum learned it that way."

"Because of *his* family?" I pressured.

"Yes... because of his family." Without saying it, Theo confirmed he knew about Callum. Perhaps everyone did... except me, of course. I was always the one who never learned the truth. They always hid everything from me.

Since taking the ship, at least June treated me like everyone else. Once she came to trust me, I suppose that was enough to see me as equal to the rest of the crew.

My attention shifted back to the deck, watching as Pickford swaggered forward to flirt with Erik, the chef. They exchanged a few laughs, then Pickford pulled a piece of chocolate from his pocket and held it out to Erik. I couldn't help but sigh. All of it seemed so natural.

"You should tell June how you feel," Theo said from behind me.

"Wha-what?!" I pivoted to glare at him.

"It's so obvious. You've been pining after her since the day you met."

"If it's so obvious, then June already knows... and she's just stringing me along. She's manipulative and—"

"She has not manipulated you. Trust me. I can tell."

I hated Theo sometimes. The way he could see straight through me made me feel naked and vulnerable like no secret could ever hide.

"June might seem strong and confident, but she is just as inexperienced in love as you."

"I doubt that."

"I know it."

"But she could have anyone. She's a captain, and she's talented and strong and...and..." I cursed under my breath. Why was I acting like this? There was no reason to be fawning after her. "I don't like her like that! This is a short-term adventure. I'm going to head home. There's no way I can feel like that about a pirate!"

"That's a lie."

"It's not—"

"It is."

I grunted, then grabbed the bottle of rum from Theo, and took a long swig.

I stayed in the crow's nest with Theo until the morning. We drank, we laughed, and we dreamt. Only when the purple dusting of dawn brushed over the Burgundy Sea, with hints of land in the distance, did I finally make my wobbly descent onto the main deck.

Each step wobbled beneath me as I strode forward, a sway in my step with each thrashing pulse of the waves. A soft headache already replaced the pulsing inebriation of the rum, and exhaustion replaced the laughter from the night.

As I wandered across the deck, I almost didn't see June as she stared out at the water. She wore her long white nightgown, her handless arm cradled against her chest, and her long black hair blowing in the wind. With my footsteps, she turned, half smiled, then returned to her watch.

"There's an inlet somewhere in this cove that we need to transverse," June said.

"We're near the treasure, then?"

"A few days away, most likely… if we can find the inlet, that is."

"I see." I stared out at the sea. Her only hand rested mere inches from mine. I was so close, I could touch it if I wanted, letting her coarse skin meet my fingers. But I didn't have the courage to touch her. Would I ever?

She was Captain June Lok; she saved us from Mr. Hackney.

I was only her pyromancer.

"You've been a huge help to me, Leena," June whispered. "Really. Thank you."

"I am doing my duty." I kept my voice level.

"You're doing more than that. You've been here…and that is more than I can say for others. It surprised me… I was sure you hated me."

"I—" I fumbled my answer. Perhaps once I hated her, but now…I couldn't say.

June cocked her head to the side, waiting.

"I thought I hated you, too," I replied.

"But you don't?"

"I wanted to; you represent everything I've hated my whole life. Piracy killed my father and took my eye…" I inhaled once before continuing. "But you stepped in to keep me from boarding the *Cobalt Hare*. You didn't even know me…and I think that says a lot about you. You saw my fear and then…acted." I clenched my hands as I continued. "I find you fascinating, and your leadership is more than I could ever ask for, if I must be honest. But...you frustrate me! I know everything you do is to keep me in check. It confuses me and leaves me reeling because all I want is to—"

I stopped myself, tears forming in my eye. I'd said too much, and June stared at me with that manipulative innocence.

"If I wanted to keep you in check, I would take out your other pretty eye there," she said without flinching. "I'm glad I don't have to 'cause I'd rather stare into your eye than the sunset."

I groaned. More tears fell down my face. "There you go again!"

"I'm only speaking the truth."

"Are you?!" I stared at her, eye to eye, every bone in my body shaking.

Her hand rose to my cheek, and with the delicacy of the wind, she cupped it. The world around me froze. The gentle movement of her hand surprised me, leaving me swooning in her grasp. With her thumb, she brushed away one of my tears.

She leaned forward, her voice soft. "Y'know, you give me hope, Leena."

"Because I can set a garden aflame?"

"No. Don't ask me to explain it…but it's you. With or without your magic. It's you."

"I…I don't know if I trust you." Every part of me wanted to give in to her, but that wall remained. She had been a part of Venom Mouth's crew when they killed my father. How could I deny that?

She released me. "Well, maybe it's time you do, Leena Davies. Otherwise, this will never work."

Before I responded, she left. What did she mean *this*? Did she mean me as a member of her crew? Or something more?

"June…" I turned to follow her.

But she had already vanished back into her cabin, leaving me with nothing more than a phantom of her hand on my cheek.

CHAPTER SIXTEEN

The Sea Serpent

Theo's shouts pulled me from my self-deprecation. The sky had turned blue, marking the passage of time. With Theo racing down from the crow's nest to ring the bell, every worry disappeared from my heart.

I spun to face him.

"Sea monster!" He shouted in my direction.

"What?!"

"There's a sea monster," he spoke, his face pale.

The crew peeked out from their different spots on the deck. Hari joined Theo's side at once. Her face darkened with protection, like when Mr. Hackney ruled the ship. Pickford bounced with excitement, with Erik and Kamalani close behind him, exchanging whispers of excitement and fear.

June hadn't reappeared.

"Are you sure it's a sea monster?" Hari asked. "Aren't they legends?"

"I thought so… but I saw it. It's larger than this ship."

"A whale?"

"No, not a whale. It was long and twisted, like a snake or a dragon or something."

"A sea serpent?" Pickford asked, still bouncing on his feet.

"Maybe. I don't know. It hasn't surfaced yet… but I saw it." Theo tapped his forehead.

We all stared amongst ourselves. Would the monster attack… if it even existed? Or would it stay, loitering beneath the waves, waiting for its prey?

Hari sank into her old role as leader. "We should be ready. If it surfaces, we cannot let it take the ship. Theo," she turned to him, "take to the crow's nest and keep an eye on it. Leena, join him. Your fire might come in handy."

"Aye," I joined Theo's side.

"Pickford, can you and Callum check if there's anything in Hackney's old library about sea monsters?"

"What!? I wanna see the beast!" Pickford argued.

"You'll be able to see it from the window. Go."

Pickford grunted.

"I'll take the harpoon. Kamalani with me!" Hari called over her shoulder to the small girl next to Pickford. "The rest of you, get to your stations."

"What about our *dear* captain?" Kamalani grumbled.

"Right… where is June?" Hari turned to me.

"I'm not her keeper," I said.

"You spend a lot of time with her—"

"I don't follow her every movement, though!"

"Fine, whatever. Get to your places. We can't risk being thrown off guard." Hari waved me off and rushed away with Kamalani toward the forward bow.

I hurried up the ladder behind Theo. Nerves shook in my hands, warming them with a hint of flame. I used all my willpower to order the flame to taper.

Fire would come later.

For now, we had to wait.

Theo analyzed the water, his eyes moving faster than a fly buzzing about the sky. I saw nothing but the waves, yet his attention did not yield. If there really was a sea monster, wouldn't it be wiser to flee? Did it remain here as a guardian for whatever treasure lay beyond the cove?

But we'd come this far. The monster couldn't stop us now.

And if I knew June well enough, she would fight it until the very end.

Besides, if Venom Mouth's treasure was just a few days away, in some ways, it was ours for the taking.

June had been part of Venom Mouth's crew.

And I had a vendetta against that pirate. Wouldn't taking the treasure be the utmost poetic revenge?

"It's right below us…" Theo mumbled.

"What? Are you sure?" I asked.

"The shadow." He pointed to the water.

I squinted, then shook my head. "I might if I had two eyes... but I see nothing."

"It's down there. Waiting. We're in its territory now." He glanced at me. "We'd be best to leave."

"I doubt June would agree."

"She's not here."

"But she's our captain." Why did I always come to her defense?

"Even so, I don't think we can fight this thing."

"Can we go around it?"

"Doubtful. It's here to protect its home. We shouldn't be here."

The boat shook with an obnoxious groan. I stumbled back and gripped the railing. The discussion ceased, and everyone on board grew quiet. It had arrived.

Beneath us, Hari readied her harpoon, attention precise as ever.

Everything froze.

A beat.

A breath.

And then a crash.

With a spout of water, a creature rose from the depths of the water. With dark skin pulsing with sea foam and mist, it slithered to the surface like a snake. Its head, with a pointed snout and deep red eyes, seemed like it belonged on the body of a mythical dragon. When it opened its mouth, it spouted out water before letting out a hiss that rumbled the entire ship.

"Sea serpent..." Theo murmured.

Pickford's shouts cut off our conversation. "It's the seagrip!" His voice carried as he raced out of Mr. Hackney's old library, a book in his hand. "The seagrip! We gotta get out of here!"

"Seagrip?" I asked Theo, my eye not leaving the monster.

It circled our ship like a cyclone, casting waves onto the deck. The crew raced to secure goods. All the while, Hari maintained her aim with the harpoon. As the serpent returned to the forward bow, Hari pulled back on the handle of the gun.

And the harpoon took aim.

The spear released.

And soared.

I held my breath as the blade pierced the skin of the seagrip.

But the monster did not flinch.

Even as more blades came flying, the seagrip continued to circle the ship, twisting and constricting, pushing us further along the current.

"We can't win against this thing!" Theo shouted.

I gripped my hands. We'd tried all our weaponry...except one. With the monster surfaced, fire could reign.

Gathering the flames on the tips of my fingers, I neared the edge of the crow's nest. The seagrip thrashed, its tail sending another wave of water onto the deck. The *Sanguine Tortuga* lurched. How much longer could the boat withstand this sort of impact?

I raised my hands as the monster rounded the aft of the ship. One shot, right in the face; surely that would be enough to end its fury and send it back into the grip of the ocean.

Fire gathered in my palms.

I aimed.

Then opened my hands.

Only to scream as I caught sight of something in the water.

"June!"

Our captain had boarded a small rowboat, and with one oar positioned clumsily against her injured arm, she paddled straight for the monster.

"June!" I cried out again. She didn't hear me.

The heat in my palms escalated, and with hands ablaze, the fire roared to life. It came from my core, funneled by my fear.

But it was too much.

Unable to control it, I sent a blast of fire above the seagrip's head.

The monster hissed again and flared its nostrils. With a splash, it avoided the flame.

Then, in one motion, it hit the pole of the crow's nest with its tail. Theo stumbled forward, hitting the wall of the crow's nest right where I'd been standing.

While I went flying into the sky.

"Leena!" I don't know who cried my name. The world spun as I toppled through the air.

I hit the body of the sea serpent with a thud. Pain cut through my chest, but I swallowed it down, using all my strength to grip the monster's scales. Up close, the serpent held a sort of menacing beauty. Its obsidian scales reflected the sky and sea, creating moments of rainbow incandescent.

Just like the *Sanguine Tortuga*.

As it moved around the ship, its muscles twisted, and its scales flared. I dug my fingers into the scales. But staying on it proved to be difficult, and every few seconds, I had to readjust.

No matter where the *Sanguine Tortuga* moved, the serpent refused to leave its side. Something compelled the monster to stay. Was it defending the treasure? Or its home?

Each time it breathed, puffs of mist and water exploded around me. I coughed, trying my best to peer through the haze. There had to be a way to stop this creature. The blades didn't pierce it, and the sea continued to beckon with its every whim.

I refocused on my hands. A distant throbbing echoed beneath my skin, begging to be set free.

My attention shifted to the ship. Hari still stood at the harpoon gun while Theo had climbed down to join Pickford. Even from a distance, their worry seeped across the water toward me.

Did I have the only chance?

I didn't know where June had disappeared to, but part of me ached for her. Why did we have to end our last discussion with such distrust?

Why couldn't I just tell her the truth?

This would be for her.

And for our crew.

I willed the fire to the surface, then, with a whisper and a prayer, sent a barrage of flames up the seagrip's spine.

The monster shrieked as the fire engulfed it.

Then, in a fit of fear and desperation, it dove back into the water headfirst. The rest of its body followed, rising into the air behind it.

Only to drag me deep beneath the water and away from those I called my home.

CHAPTER SEVENTEEN

Where Loyalty Forms

First came the water.

Then the darkness.

Followed by a cough.

The cough raced through my body, waking me with a gasp of air. I still couldn't see anything. First, I felt the heat battering down above me. Then, the sand cradling my body.

When my vision finally stabilized, I caught a glimpse of the sun winking down at me, blinding me with its rude light and threatening to take out my other eye.

Was this death?

If it was, it smelled like the sea.

Slowly, I tried sitting up, only for pressure to sink into my chest and force me back onto the ground. I cursed, then coughed up phlegm.

"Don't move. You broke your ribs."

If my chest didn't hurt, I might have jumped in surprise. June sat next to me, combing her drenched hair with

198

her good hand. Just past her, nothing more than a blur, the rowboat bobbed against the coastline. The shadow of the *Sanguine Tortuga* moved along the horizon in the distance.

I refocused on June. "What happened?"

"You took a tumble into the water. Thought you drowned, but got you out of there. The waves took us into this here inlet. Pretty sure the monster traveled down that way." She motioned toward a narrow channel weaving through the beach.

"Then shouldn't we get out of here?"

"Well, my boat's got a leak, and the Tortuga can't dock on the sandbar here. Pretty sure she's going to take the long way around. I say, once you're up for it, we go follow that sea serpent."

"Follow it?!" It hurt to protest, another jab of pain making a home in my chest.

"Calm down. You probably broke a rib or something. Here, let me look." June moved closer to me and took the edge of my shirt with her good hand. My entire body froze as she slowly lifted my blouse up a few inches. She took her thumb and pressed it against the blue bruise on my side.

I cursed under my breath.

"Mhm. You broke something there. Not much we can do until we're back on the Tortuga. Just gotta take it easy." She let my shirt fall. As her fingers moved away, I exhaled.

The world stopped spinning, and despite the gnawing pain, I could think again. June continued, "We're going to need to move soon. Tide's coming in."

"Oh. Okay…" I tried to sit up again, only for my body to seep back into the sand.

"Wait, a few minutes at least. You did almost die."

I didn't argue, sinking deeper into the sand. June didn't budge from beside me, her gaze unyielding. What went through her head? Every moment, she calculated something; every movement came with reason. If she saved me, the question came: why?

I didn't take long for her to speak again.

"When you were on the ship, you had fire ready," she said.

"Yes. I was going to attack."

"But you missed."

"Yes…"

"Was it on purpose?"

I nodded.

"Why?"

I turned away from her. "I didn't want you to be collateral damage."

"How come? You don't trust me. Didn't you want to protect your friends?"

"Yes, but...I didn't want to hurt you." I gulped, letting the words sit. I felt naked to her stare; she could read me like a book.

And I hated it.

"Why not? You've said yourself that you hate pirates and don't trust me." June kept pressuring.

I shot a glance back at her. What could I say? How could I win this battle?

"I saved you..." I started, letting the words hang before continuing, "for the same reason you saved me today."

She stared at me. I expected her to say something snarky or something about my flame. But she really seemed to stare at me, analyzing my every move, looking deep into my soul. Her response came as nothing more than a whisper. "You're my first mate. Can't let anything bad happen to you."

I leaned back on my shoulders, "You said that once before... that I'm your first mate. Wouldn't Hari be the better choice? She's been around longer."

"Hari's a good quartermaster and boatswain but not what I need in a first mate. I need my first mate to be...someone who actually asks questions."

"Sounds annoying."

"It is necessary, though."

"But what does that matter if I don't trust you?"

"I guess that's a good thing. Means if I decide to go rogue, someone might stop me." She winked.

I still didn't understand her rationale. "I doubt I'll make a good first mate. It just doesn't make sense."

"You already have, though."

"What?"

"You heard me."

We stared at each other. Me... a first mate? Me... actually useful? I never imagined that this would be my life. Perhaps I made a decent enough pirate...

My head spun. No, I said one adventure! I wasn't going to be a pirate.

After all, pirates killed my father.

Pirates took my eye.

But I stared at June, and my heart swooned. Her tenacity and bravery, her leadership and guile; she may have scared me, but she was everything and a true leader.

And part of me would go to the end of the world with her.

"I guess we'll see how it plays out, then?" I asked her.

She smiled slightly. "Yeah... one step at a time."

June helped me off the sandbar, her arm laced around my waist. My heart thudded beneath her grip. Her touch was gentle but firm, keeping me upright as we walked.

I tried to distract myself by talking. "Why did you disembark and go after the monster?"

"Thought I could attack it from the belly. I might only have one hand, but I can wield my daggers good enough." June tightened her grip around my waist.

"It was huge!"

"I've seen bigger."

"What? Where?"

"Well, not those kinds of beasts... but others back home."

"Like what?"

She smiled to herself before saying, "Sīchóu Shíyóu was once the land of giants and supposed mythical creatures. Everything is bigger there."

"Giants are myths."

"So are sea serpents." Her eyes met mine with that distant twinkle. "There aren't giants anymore... at least not like the ones that reached the moon. But their remnants remain. You should see the structures back home. They towered higher than the clouds."

"You're lying."

"Maybe I'll get to show you someday." She kept her gaze on me.

It remained tight like a lock, unwavering. I could bask in her eyes for hours; they captured the stars with twinkling light.

"I'd like that," I whispered, unable to turn away from her.

"So you're saying you'll be my first mate?"

"I'm saying…I might be willing to go on more than one adventure."

"Even if I'm a pirate?"

"What is a pirate but a name?" I asked, reciting what she and Hari had once said to me.

"Is it not violence and plundering?"

"Maybe…" I let my eye lose focus, staring past June at the shifting sea. Yes, the past couple of weeks saw nothing more than violence and plundering, but I also saw the person behind each action. June acted with accord. "But… at first, I might have overlooked the reason."

She scowled, loosening her grip around me. What did I say? I thought that was what she wanted to hear. But she didn't reply at all, walking forward along the coastline, attention trailing out to the water where our ship continued to circle the island.

"I'm not a good person, Leena." June finally said.

I glanced at her. "I know."

She stepped back, cocking her head. "And you'd still be my first mate?"

I followed her gaze out to sea. Over the past few years, with Mr. Hackney, with my mother, and now with June, I'd learned one truth. It took me a while to accept it.

But after June saved me, and after I saved her, there was one fundamental answer: "I don't think there are any good people. So I might as well spend time with those who matter to me."

"Earlier today, you said you didn't trust me."

I cursed and threw back my head. Why did she have to bring that up again? Couldn't we forget that conversation?

As I stomped forward, I lost my footing, collapsing on the ground with a groan.

"Leena!" June raced toward me.

I held out my hand to stop her. I wanted to get my point across to her. "Earlier today, I was scared. My emotions made little sense. Trust is such a strong word, and I wasn't certain how I felt. But... I *do* trust you'll defend those you care about."

"And do you trust I care about you?"

"Do you?"

"I asked you first," June stepped toward me.

"Well, I won't humiliate myself with the answer."

"And you think I want to?"

"I think you're braver than I am."

"Not in manners like this." June sat down across from me so our knees touched.

With my hands shaking, I placed a palm on her knee. "Then let us say it at the same time."

"Answer if we trust each other?" She didn't flinch at my touch.

"Yes. Answer the question in three… two… one…"

And in a single breath, we both spoke the same words, so they echoed across the beach in a gasp of wind.

"I do."

We fell asleep inland on the island, using the sand as a bed and palm fronds as blankets. June slept less than a foot away from me. It was out in the open now: the words of trust and respect. But we said no more, letting the night take away our truths, and morning welcomed us with a soft hello. We said not a word. A declaration of trust; it seemed to lock us in like a prayer.

And even without opening our hearts further, as we walked toward the southern coast of the island, it was with our shoulders closer and hands brushing as we walked. I still didn't have the guile to tell her the extensive nature of my emotions; I didn't dare tell her the strange fantasies that filled my head or how she lingered in my dreams.

Trust. That was the first step.

At least for me.

We followed the inlet further into the island. Part of me wondered if the *Sanguine Tortuga* would be able to find us. With Theo on board, they were bound to know, but the uncertainty remained about when, where, and how. What if they decided June and I weren't worth it? What if they committed treason and took the ship for their own use?

June didn't seem phased, striding ahead with confidence, her hair caught by the occasional wisp of the wind. Every now and again, she paused at the inlet, observing the ripples of the waters.

"What are you looking for?" I asked her.

"Signs of the sea monster."

"In this small of a stream?"

"Ay. It's like a tunnel, see?" She motioned to the riverbank. "I think it made this stream."

"So the stream will lead us to the treasure?"

"It might. If not… at least to the other side of the island."

I didn't question her judgment. If she had traveled with Venom Mouth for all those years, then surely, she knew some signs of this mysterious treasure. I could feel it in my chest, thumping. Were we close? What would it be?

Initially, I made the claim of water. But Pickford was right—there were far greater mysteries out there. If the seagrip showed us anything, it was that magic hid even in the murkiest waters, and things we never knew existed would someday rise from the abyss beneath our boat.

Pickford had told so many stories. He mentioned a fountain of youth, sirens, dragons, and more. While I knew it might be nothing more than a chest of gold and jewels, or even a crystal-clear lake, my mind exploded with the possibilities.

If June and I found it together, wouldn't it be ours to share?

Yes, it would be for our crew, but it would be *our* treasure. Just like it had been Venom Mouth's treasure.

"What do you think the treasure is?" I asked June. "You heard my idea... but you never said yours."

"To be frank, I don't think there is a treasure," June said.

"What?" That shocked me. We had been venturing specifically to this treasure; June fixated on that map. How could there not be a treasure?

"Venom Mouth wasn't one to plunder for riches. That's why I'm shocked they even had a map."

"But aren't pirates all about treasure?"

"Not Venom Mouth. They wanted to prove a point."

"And what was that point?"

"That no one rules these seas, and anyone who claimed to do so deserved a wad of venom to the face."

"Then..." I raised my hand to my eyepatch, "Why did they spit on me?"

"Honestly? You probably got in the way. They didn't really want to harm children."

"Then what were they doing on Janis?"

"I don't know. Honestly don't even remember if I was on board at that point. The years all blend together…" June glanced at me. She reached for my eyepatch and slowly lowered it. I didn't flinch but stood there, waiting for her to cringe at the burns on my face. "You should wear that scar with pride. Not everyone can say they met Venom Mouth and lived."

"My mother always had me hide it…" I whispered, bringing my hand to her hand. "I think it reminded her of what happened to my father."

"But I can't imagine that was your fault."

"I wandered out that night. I wasn't supposed to, but I did. And my father followed." I licked my bottom lip and looked away from her. As her hand fell, I pulled the eyepatch back over my eye. "I was supposed to be Venom Mouth's victim, not him."

"Why would Venom Mouth care about a child?"

"I, um, am unsure."

"Chances are, they hoped someone more important would come with a child's scream. Venom Mouth tried to avoid harming children. Most of the time, they had a vendetta to fill. I'm sure Janis had something they wanted… or a point they wanted to prove."

"Just like you have a vendetta?"

June smirked before saying, "Being taken from your home at a young age leaves you with one."

"Why not just go home then?" I asked.

"Sīchóu Shíyóu is a long voyage away from here. Perhaps I'll return home someday, but I doubt my family is still there. They never sought me out."

"When were you taken?" I wanted to learn everything about June, but part of me worried one wrong question would push her away.

Yet, to my surprise, she answered, "I was a young kid, probably five or six years of age, when the *Commeant* came. Not sure why they took me, but they did. They took everything from me. I can't even speak Sī yǔ... only know how to read it. Tried to relearn it after Venom Mouth freed me a few years later, but it never came back."

"So instead, you learned how to be a pirate?"

"Venom Mouth taught me how to never accept a fate I didn't want. Yes, Theo always talks about the things he sees, but I don't believe any of that is definite. No, I will decide my future, not some petty magic or hand of a so-called god."

I kept prying. "Do you believe in a god?"

"Not anymore." She punctuated the statement with a huff, and I knew I should stop pressuring her.

We continued in silence. My ribs no longer hurt as badly, more a constant throbbing than the sharp pain of the day before, but I still welcomed June's support. Despite her droll nature, she always made sure I was okay.

The statements came short and abrupt, but it was enough for me to know that she didn't just trust me... but she cared.

Even if it was in her own way.

Before crossing a dune, we both removed our boots, letting the white sand sink between our toes. Its warmth soothed the calluses on my feet, and as we walked, it brought me back to the island with my brother, where we used to play and laugh.

I glanced at June as we reached the top of the dune. "I'll race you to the bottom."

"Are you mad? You have broken ribs!"

"Then you shouldn't have to worry."

Before she replied, I bounded down the side of the dune. It hurt to breathe. But as I raced down, I let the wind catch me, and it became an easy descent. June followed right on my heels, her soft chuckles following me. For a moment, I had no worried again, and all that mattered was June and me running along the beach. In another life, would we have met like this? Would we have been friends or more, not with some strange goal of finding an un-known treasure? What would we share other than death? A favorite food? Inside jokes? A life untainted?

I could only let these dreams carry me to the bottom of the dune, where a field of red flowers waited for us. There, June crashed into me with a laugh.

She caught my hand before I toppled to the ground. "You alright there? Don't want to break you anymore."

"Yeah, yeah, I'm fine. Thank you."

June pulled me forward, staring hard at me for a second. It was again that analytical look, the one that bore deep into me, deciphering each of my freckles and scars. This time, I didn't turn from her.

I trusted her.

I followed her.

And I suppose, perhaps, I adored her.

Did I love her? That would be a rash thing to say. But I adored her and would protect her, my captain, no matter the outcome.

Her attention drifted away from me, and she whispered, "Leena... look."

I turned.

Before us, the seagrip waited in a lake full of silver.

CHAPTER EIGHTEEN

The Silver Lake

T he lake glimmered as we approached, basking in the blood-red coloration of the surrounding flowers. All the while, the seagrip hissed, sending ripples across the strange silver water as it watched us.

"Be careful. That thing is not happy." June whispered beside me.

"Yeah, I get that."

I kept my gaze focused on the monster. Its long body shifted, each scale reflective of the colors surrounding it. It reminded me of June. I couldn't pull my gaze away from it. The seagrip returned my gaze, its red eyes baring into my soul as if reading me like Theo.

A beat passed.

Then the seagrip lunged forward, extending its fangs, before diving beneath the surface of the strange lake. Its tail flicked once before it descended, and for a moment, all remained calm. I stepped back, clutching June's wrist, holding my breath.

The seagrip emerged from the water again, dripping with silver from its scales, its red eyes gleaming in fury. Another hiss escaped its expansive jaw.

"We're gonna have to kill it if we want that treasure," June muttered.

"But what *is* the treasure?"

"Must be that lake."

"But what's so special about it?"

"Well, it's made of silver. Or something like silver." June stepped forward to examine it, but the seagrip let out another loud hiss. She stumbled back, then reached for the dagger in her boot.

"Don't be ridiculous! You can't just stab it!" I shouted.

"Watch me." She raced toward the water and, despite my protests, leapt into the lake. The silver liquid engulfed her at once. I screamed her name again, but she didn't surface.

The seagrip thrashed.

"Stop! Stop!" I screamed.

The seagrip didn't budge.

"We're here because of Venom Mouth!" I said.

If the monster understood me, it showed no signs.

I continued, "Venom Mouth is dead... but we're here in their place."

The monster slowed its rumbles, its red eyes watching me with curiosity. I only prayed that it understood.

But more, I prayed June would escape the depths of the water beneath it.

My fingers trembled as I removed my eyepatch, "Venom Mouth marked me so we could find you." It was a lie, really. But the monster didn't know that. "The girl beneath the waves right now... that's Venom Mouth's daughter. We are here in their stead."

The seagrip analyzed my movements, its large head bobbing up and down with the waves. Along its backside, June resurfaced, silver dripping from her hair. She climbed out of the water like a siren, gripping the seagrip's scales and ascending its long tail. The beast flicked its tail once, but to my relief, she held onto its back with dexterity. How she did so with just one hand, I did not know, but she moved along it, one hand as an anchor, each boot as her weights. The dagger glimmered from its place in her mouth.

I approached the edge of the silver lake, still with my gaze on the seagrip. It flared its nostrils once. "You must be tired from defending this lake. It's time to rest." I knelt before the lake and cupped my hand. The liquid moved like water, but it weighed heavy, like gold. As I stared at it, it didn't reflect the sky. In some ways, it reflected different moments or visions or *something* just beneath the surface.

Was it magic?

As I removed my hand from the water, the beast lurched, a screech escaping its mouth. I stumbled back as it thrashed, sending a wave of the silver liquid in my direction. My fear took me by force, and as it spun its tail around, a blaze of fire escaped my fingers.

"June! Watch out!" I shouted as the fire blasted toward the monster.

She didn't even flinch as she reached the top of the seagrip. Standing on its head, she pulled the dagger from her mouth. I could tell she said something, but the words did not reach me.

She lifted the dagger in the air.

And stabbed the seagrip in the eye.

The monster cried out and swayed, but June remained on its head. She moved with precision, locking me in a trance, as she removed the dagger from the monster's eye and stabbed the other one in a fluid motion.

The monster thrashed. June kept her hand looped around the dagger, and as it thrashed, she held on as the blade cut open the side of the monster's face. Black blood seeped from the wound, dripping into the silver lake, casting shadows that looked like sirens and mermaids wandering beneath the surface.

As the blade reached the edge of the seagrip's upper lip, June lost her grip on the dagger. The monster churned and opened its mouth. June fell forward, landing straight on the monster's tongue.

"June!" I shouted.

She didn't hear me, stumbling to her feet. Slowly, she turned.

Then the seagrip closed its mouth.

And swallowed.

"No! June!" With every drop of fury in my blood, with every sensation of heat and every lack of mercy, I opened my palms. The fire moved with my emotions, and with a single gasp, another fireball swarmed from my fingertips. It raced through the air, and I prayed it would land where I had ordered it.

Never had fire moved so slow.

I held my breath, waiting.

Then it hit the seagrip in the face.

The seagrip shrieked, its body thrashing, flinging scales across the lake. It sent a gust of wind in my direction with the scales, and my eyepatch came loose. I didn't fix it, fascinated as the monster writhed. It almost appeared like the monster melted, its skin peeling away, dripping off its bones like the lake beneath it.

Only did its skeleton remain.

As the bones fell, I raced into the water. Amongst those bones had to be June. She couldn't be gone. Not now. Not after we found the treasure.

I swam forward, "June! June... where are you!? June!"

"Leena!"

Her voice sent shivers down my spine. I continued forward, listening to her calls, begging for her voice.

Was it in my imagination?

"Leena! Over here!"

She clung to a rib from the beast with her single hand. Even drenched in the entrails of the monster, with silver and red hanging from her head, in that moment, I swore she never looked more beautiful.

I swam to June in haste and helped her from the rib. With my arm around her waist, we floated there for a moment.

"Good job, first mate," she whispered.

"I wasn't going to lose my captain."

"I guess we're even then, aren't we?"

"For now."

As the seagrip continued its disintegration, we hurried back to shore. I didn't let go of June until we hit the shoreline, where we both rolled onto our backs and exhaled in unison.

What would I have done if I lost her? She was my captain and my friend.

And I hadn't told her the depths of my feelings.

I had yet to tell her how confused she made me. Ever since I first met her, she sent my heart into a flurry and my mind in circles. None of it made sense.

But had any of this?

We went from slaves to pirates in a blink.

Perhaps that was how love worked. One moment, you saw a person.

The next, you would die for them.

"June..." I said as I sat up from the ground.

"Hm?" She glanced at me.

"I... um... I..." I cursed. What was I going to say? What was I supposed to do?

The little courage I had took control of me, and I reached for her face and kissed her.

And she kissed me back with the power of the sea.

CHAPTER NINETEEN

The Treasure

J une and I sat by the edge of the silver lake, surrounded by the red flowers, letting our breathing settle while stealing an occasional touch or kiss. With a single movement, our walls had fallen. Our touches stayed innocent, but if a smile brought me to paradise, then I would bask in it. June had locked me in her grasp when she first came aboard, but now I stood at the same level.

And she saw me the same.

After catching our breaths, June approached the silver lake.

"Bet the *Tortuga* has made dock somewhere. We should get going..." June said.

I didn't argue, instead joining her side. The silver lake bubbled, and in each pop, I swore images filled its surface. For one moment, I saw a city against a red sea; in another, a dragon flying through the sky; in the next, a field of red flowers. I could stare at it for hours, but June pulled me away.

"But is this the treasure?" I asked, "Or something else?"

"Not sure... but I bet I know someone who will," June remarked as she put the canteen on her belt.

"Theo?" I asked.

"Mhm. Our little seer will know for sure."

"He's not that little. He's seventeen!"

"But he's the youngest on the ship."

"By one year!"

"Doesn't matter." June waltzed forward, only stopping to lift one of the seagrip's ribs from the ground. She jabbed it forward like a sword, smiled, then continued.

I followed in a rush. "What're you doing with that?"

"Not sure yet. I'll see what I can do."

"New sword?"

"Nah. Gotta be something better than that." June examined the bone.

I didn't want her to settle back into silence. Questions continued to escape. "Why do you think that seagrip was guarding the lake?"

"Well, it's obviously some magic or something. I feel like I remember Venom Mouth holding a flask of it or something. Might have had something to do with their venom mouth." She snorted.

"I'm guessing you never asked?"

"I knew better than to ask. Just observed."

"That's why you're good at that now?"

"Guess so." June hopped over a piece of driftwood.

I continued to press, "What was it like aboard Venom Mouth's ship?"

She slowed and glanced at me. "After being aboard a slave ship, it was freeing. I could be... *me*. Didn't need to bite my tongue. Got to learn to wield a dagger. And I got to learn about the world. Venom Mouth did bad things, but they took good care of their crew. I might not be their daughter, but they considered everyone on board their children."

"It's hard to imagine..." I reached for my scarred eye. In the scuffle with the seagrip, I lost my eyepatch.

"Again, can't answer why they attacked you... but it doesn't mean they didn't care about their crew. People are complex."

"Yes, but you can't expect me to sing praises for Venom Mouth."

"I'd be concerned if you did."

"Just like I'd be concerned if you started saying good things about Mr. Hackney and Ms. Platt."

"There ain't nothing good to say about them. They promise you the world, but at what cost?"

"You've shown me more of the world in the past few weeks than Hackney ever did."

"Well, that's my job." June smirked back at me.

My heart lurched, but my head kept me in line. I didn't want to ruin whatever *this* was by acting too eager for June. One step at a time… we would take one step at a time.

June slowed her pace. "I hear the ocean. Can't be far now."

The sound of the waves thrashing pushed through the grasses and the few trees.

We hurried along the sand. The first sign of the ocean came with not the water, not the waves, but with a shadow extending higher than the treetops, in a dark shadow.

"There she is," June whispered.

And there she stood, waiting for us like June promised: our ship, our home, the *Sanguine Tortuga*.

Hari sprinted toward us along the coast, her long black hair catching in the wind. Her smile spread from cheek to cheek.

"You're okay!" She threw her arms around me.

"Of course I am." I smiled.

"But you were attacked by the seagrip!"

"No, that was—" Then I remembered. It felt already like a lifetime ago that I'd last been on board the *Sanguine Tortuga*. That was the whole reason June and I ended up on this island after all—I had fallen off the ship.

But the monster had eaten June.

I glanced back at June. She fiddled with the rib bone. What was it like inside the monster's belly? I hadn't even asked her. When she survived, I was too excited to think.

But now… would she think of me as heartless? Selfish even?

The worries I once had over June's heartlessness vanished, replaced instead by new worries: that I instead would fail her.

"Are you okay? You two are getting along, right?" Hari pulled me back to the present.

"What? No. We're fine."

"I think they're more than fine." Theo came up behind Hari, smirking.

"Stay out of it," I hissed.

He kept on with that ridiculous smile.

Hari turned to face him. "I thought you were staying on board."

"Eh, figured I'd come say hi to Leena. They probably need me."

"Why would we—"

June cut me off, "Love that intuition of yours, Theo. C'mon. Gotta show you something."

"Wait! You just got back!" Hari called.

"Won't take long. C'mon, Leena!"

I smiled sheepishly at Hari, then hurried behind June and Theo. Without a doubt, Hari would interrogate me later, but I wanted to hear what Theo thought of the pool. He was the only one who might understand it. To the rest of us, it was nothing more than magical goo.

Theo didn't ask questions as June led us back toward the silver lake. My calves ached as I rushed behind them. My ribs ached with each breath. But I didn't slow. What did our treasured pool hold for us?

June continued marching ahead. She wore her excitement close, but now and then, she would glance in my direction with that smile.

It didn't take as long to get back to the pool. The trek to the shoreline had taken what felt like hours, but really, it took no time at all. Once you learn the way of the water, all you have to do is follow the current back to where it all started.

Theo slowed his approach as we neared the pool, moving slow and steady amongst the red flowers. He approached it with hesitancy, brow furrowed as he knelt before it and placed his fingers above the water. June and I remained quiet, waiting for something miraculous to occur.

"Well?" June pressured.

Theo didn't respond, directing his fingers to the surface of the liquid. "Fascinating… this pool is powerful…"

"And?" June asked.

"I—I—" Theo's face paled.

A pause.

His red eyes widened.

Then he collapsed face-first into the silver liquid.

"You mean the *treasure* did this to Theo!?" Hari exclaimed.

June and I had dragged Theo's unconscious body away from the silver pool and back to the ship. Onboard, Hari fawned like a mother hen, rushing to get Theo into his bed. Pickford abandoned his card game with a few other crewmates and rushed to Theo's side. The two of them acted like a set of parents, checking Theo's pulse, getting him water, and tucking him into bed. In his room, they treated him like a fallen prince.

But outside in the hall, Hari roared at June like a monsoon.

"How was I supposed to know he would have some strange magic reaction to it?" June scoffed, playing with the seagrip rib bone.

"I don't know! But you should have watched him."

"He's sixteen. He's got a mind of his own."

"And now he's in a coma!"

"You don't know that."

"This is irresponsible, June! He's part of your crew."

"And he'll wake up. But we can't sit here waiting for that. We gotta empty some barrels so we can fill them with the silver water."

"You still want to take it!?"

"Absolutely. It sure could give us a pretty penny. You'd be surprised what people might do to get hold of magic."

Hari threw her head back and groaned. I kept to the side, watching. June and I had touched the lake, and nothing happened. Perhaps it acted as a protector against magic.

No, that wouldn't make sense. *I* had magic.

But Theo had sight.

What did he see? What caused him to fall?

Pickford must have been thinking the same thing. "He probably saw something when he touched it. We should probably wait until Theo wakes up... so he can tell us what he saw. This must be some special magic or something."

"We don't have time." June snapped.

"What? Why!? We have all the time in the world! It's not like we have anywhere to go after this." Pickford said.

June narrowed her eyes. "We *do not* have time to dilly dally. Remember, we took this ship, and *we* killed Bernard Hackney. I am sure someone is tracking us. It will just be a matter of time until they catch up. And without our little seer conscious, I won't have a clue when they're coming."

"We had a hard enough time finding this spot—"

"But we have a very recognizable ship."

Hari sucked in her lips, glanced between Pickford and me, then said, "We'll put it to a vote."

"This isn't a democracy."

"It is *our* ship. We vote."

June glowered at Hari. I thought for a moment she might shank her with the rib bone. But they remained locked in a standoff. Pickford leaned against the wall with his arms crossed. His attention kept darting back to Theo's room.

I clenched my fist. Why did they have to argue over this? We couldn't have our ship divided—not when we might finally have enough riches to be free.

"What about a compromise?" I interjected.

"Like what?" June asked without looking at me.

"How about we stay for three days? If Theo wakes up, we'll find out what he has to say. If he doesn't, then well… we take however many barrels of the silver liquid and sail out of this cove. That way… we all get what we want. Plus… I'm sure everyone wants a chance to see the island and all."

June and Hari continued their glowering.

"One week," Hari said, unflinching.

"Three days," June replied.

"Five."

"Two."

"Fine! I'll take three." Hari threw her hands up in the air. "Three days and no less."

"Very well. And I'll be watching." June left without another word, still clinging to her seagrip rib.

Hari turned her attention to me. "Why are you on her side here? I thought Theo was your friend."

I opened my mouth, only for Pickford to interject.

"Because I'm sure we'll find Captain Lok and Miss Davies up in the crow's nest later." He chuckled.

My face warmed.

Hari shook her head. "You could do better, Leena. June isn't a good person."

I kept my head low and my voice lower. "Neither are we."

But Hari didn't hear me, already turning her attention to Theo's room to do whatever *good* still existed aboard the *Sanguine Tortuga*.

CHAPTER TWENTY

Sail Away

June spent most of the next three days locked away in the captain's quarters. During the day, I completed my duties on board, ignoring the glares from Hari. Her judgment left me feeling nauseous. The last thing I wanted was to disappoint her.

At least Pickford and Callum treated me with the same regard. They smiled each day, passed jokes at mealtime, and checked that I was doing well enough. But Theo's empty presence loomed. The crow's nest remained empty. Without Theo, I lost my confidante and friend.

Please wake up soon, Theo. I prayed as I worked.

Well, until the evening, when I abandoned my duties to slip into the captain's quarters. The first night, June didn't move from her desk, whittling away at the seagrip's rib. On the table behind her, staring out at sea, sat that pearl camellia from São Caméliosa.

I didn't question her, sitting there in comfortable silence in the chair across from her. At first, I wasn't sure if she even wanted me there. So I spent the time sitting there, pondering my future. I hadn't put my eyepatch back on yet, so I held it there in my hand, debating its place now that I had exposed my truths.

"Keep it off," June said. "Wear your scar with pride."

I placed the eye patch on the desk.

Then she touched my leg with her bare foot and smirked.

The next day, she greeted me at the door, then led me across the room to where she'd been working on the seagrip's rib. In its place stood not the rib but a polished fixture shaped like a hook.

"What'd you think?" she asked.

"What is it?"

"My new hand, of course."

"Your... new hand?"

"Yes, that's right."

"But how are you going to attach it?"

"I'm sure there's someone in Triguá who's got some sort of contraption." She paced around her piece of art, smiling. "Figured what else to carve my hand from but the monster my first mate killed?"

"I didn't mean to... it was just a reaction."

"You saved my life. That thing ate me." She winked.

The next question slipped from my lips. She hadn't spoken of the seagrip's attack since it occurred, and now, I had to ask the question. "What was that like?"

June stared at the rib, poked at it once, then said, "It was like… sliding down a muddy road… but dark and endless. I used my dagger to cling to the wall of its neck… but in those few moments, I had to come to terms with my death." She raised her eyes to mine. "Glad I didn't. I'm not gonna die by some petty sea snake."

I leaned against the desk. "And how would you want to die?"

"Honestly, I don't care, as long as I outlive all the ones who've done me wrong."

"You have a list?"

"All up here." She tapped her head. "And trust me, I'm gonna live a long while with how long this list is."

"Well, that's good… because…" My cheeks warmed. "I don't want you going anywhere."

"I'm not leaving your side. Well, unless you have a plan to die early." She stared at me, analyzing every move as she approached me.

"No… not really. My death would be…" What would my death be? I'd never really thought of it. "I guess it would be… with whoever I loved by my side."

"So we'll go down together then?" June stepped toward me. "Or do you have someone else in mind?"

My first thought fled to Tristan. When I was young, I never imagined leaving his side. Now, here stood June, the woman who made my heart patter; for all I knew, I might never see Tristan again.

"We'll go down together," I replied.

June returned that sentiment with a kiss.

The morning of the third day arrived, and Theo did not wake. June took her chance then, ordering the strongest of us to roll barrels to the silver lake and fill as many as possible before the sun set. The moment the moon rose to the highest point in the sky that night, she aimed to leave and head toward Triguá. She didn't give anyone a reason for her destination, but I guessed it was for her hook.

While June commanded most of the crew to carry barrels back to shore, I tended to Theo. He still slept, with sweat matting his hair, jaw clenched. Callum sat on the other side of the bed, reading one of his history books. Hari stopped by once to change out Theo's bedpan but otherwise said nothing.

I sighed as she left.

Callum heard me, "She's not upset with you."

"Then why won't she talk to me?"

"She's worried about Theo... frustrated with June... and concerned for you."

"Concerned for me?"

"June's dangerous. She's worried that you've been blindsided."

"I know June's dangerous—"

"She's out for herself. You've seen how she behaves."

"She has more to her than that."

"You're smitten."

"You're Mr. Hackney's son! He probably... manipulated your point of view or something!"

Callum shook his head and closed the book. "My father never had a conversation with me about June Lok. But he's dead now, so I can't ask him, anyway."

"She's our captain—"

"Everyone feels this way, Leena. June is dangerous. She's liberating... but dangerous. Just be careful. She'd sooner sell you for a new ship than keep you by her side."

I turned away from him. "You don't know her."

"Do you?"

"Better than you!" I started toward the exit. As I reached the door, I paused, turning to face him again. "If this is how Hari feels, she can say it outright to me. I'm not the same *child* she met those years ago. Just because June wears her sins on her sleeves, it doesn't mean we're better than her. We all have our demons."

Callum didn't say a word, head hanging low, the book still clenched in his hands. Whether he wanted to admit it, we were all pirates here; none of us had a clean pallet. Blood rested on our hands; it was a first deed, but it wouldn't be our last.

I started to leave once again, only for Theo's voice to pull me back to the present.

"June will not be the traitor," he whispered from the bed.

"Theo!?" I raced to his side.

But he still hadn't woken, with only his voice drifting as a phantom in the air.

I watched as June directed the barrels onboard as the sun made its final descent over the island. She collected over a dozen barrels, each secured with a tight lid. The crew returned stained with silver, but no one else had a reaction like Theo. Rather, there seemed to be a new excitement. The crew grinned amongst each other, with Pickford's laughter carrying them on board.

Once the last barrel reached the gangway, I hurried downstairs to help June. She paced along the barrels, tapping each one as she counted them repeatedly.

"Everyone seems in better spirits," I remarked.

"Once they saw this magical liquid, their mood changed. Not sure what it is about this stuff or what is so special about it in the first place, but it's got something that someone will want. Why else would Venom Mouth care about it?"

"True…" I placed my hand on the barrel. "How are we going to offload it, though?"

June picked at the wood of the barrel. "I know Triguá has a large magical base. Hoping someone there will see potential in it."

"Got it." I kicked the ground. The discussion I had with Callum remained in my head. Would June sell me for a chance of riches? Or was Theo's unconscious prediction true? Did that even have to do with me?

June approached me. "You're thinking. I don't like when you think. You start to ask questions."

I sighed. "Callum was trying to get in my head. Gave me warnings about you."

"I've given you warnings about me. What's the problem?"

Slowly, I raised my head. "He said you would sell me if the opportunity presented itself."

June stepped back. "And you believe him?"

I raised my hands. "No! Absolutely not! I defended you to the grave."

She didn't reply.

"I just… was wondering… why would he think that?"

"Cause it's what his father would do." June ran her hand over the wall of the ship. "He would sell anyone for riches. But if there's one thing I'm not, it's a slave trader."

"Of course you're not."

June was so much more than that. Did she kill? Yes, but always with cause. Did she fight? Absolutely. Did she steal? Of course.

And I was her first mate. So my job would be to defend her.

"C'mon, let's get this ship ready for sailing. The last thing I need is Hari trying to derail this whole thing."

"She won't derail this," I replied.

"I don't know… she doesn't seem all too happy with the circumstances. Plus, she's got some pull. I don't need a riot."

"Well…" I took her hand as we climbed up the stairs, "if they try to stop you, at least you have me… right?"

"Now's not the time for romance."

"No. I mean…" I opened my free hand and let a flame ignite in my palm, "you have your pyromancer."

June stared at the flame, then smiled. "We can burn whoever stands in our way."

Triguá

Life on board returned to normal. We completed our daily tasks with vigor, ate our meals with jeers, and spent the nights living our stolen lives with glee. For me, that meant spending the evenings in June's office. Some nights, we didn't even speak; June sat there reading through some of Mr. Hackney's old papers. Others, we filled the void with the truths of our past or at least those we wished to share. And on a select few nights, we kissed and touched with innocence.

My early dreams had involved June taking control of me, holding me down as she bent me to her whims. Yet, in reality, she operated with the same hesitancy as me. She took care with each touch, proceeded slowly with each movement, and never asked for more than a pious stroke. Sometimes, I wished it would take hold of me like the June in my dreams. But the tenderness was almost... well... sweet.

One evening, I found her sitting at Mr. Hackney's desk, reading through Mr. Hackney's papers. She didn't look up as I entered, fidgeting with the pearl camellia in her hand. I took a seat on the bench by the wall. Her eyes darted back and forth along the page, a frown on her lips as she read the document.

After a few minutes, she straightened out the papers, then held them out to me. "I think these belong to you."

I carefully took them. My heart dropped at the writing: my letters to Tristan.

"He never sent them…" I whispered.

"Did you honestly expect him to?"

"I guess not…" But part of me had hoped, when I was younger, that he had sent all these letters to my brother. What did he think now? Did he think I abandoned him? That I ran away? What would my mother tell him?

"He has letters for everyone here. Didn't send a single one." June motioned to the stack of letters beside her.

I traced my handwriting with my finger. So many of us had placed our hopes in Mr. Hackney that maybe one letter would reach our loved ones. What did he do with these instead? Read over them and laugh? Use them to kindle his fire? None of my letters were missing… but it didn't mean others didn't end up in flame.

The edge of my papers caught fire. I stifled it at once, then turned back to June. "I can deliver the letters to the crew."

"Is it really worth our time?"

I glanced at my letters again. "Yes. It will... remove any doubt that Mr. Hackney was a bad man. The last thing we need is uncertainty and disloyalty."

"I like the way you think."

"That's why I'm your first mate."

It took me all night to deliver the letters. Sure, I'd been on this ship for years, but I still never committed to memory where everyone slept. After we rid ourselves of Mr. Hackney, everyone changed their sleeping arrangements as well.

Most of the crew didn't seem shocked when I delivered the letters. A few stared at the pages, their eyes dropping in defeat. Pickford crumpled his letters and threw them into the sea. Callum pocketed his letters like any other message. I even left Theo's letters by his bed, but he still hadn't woken. Hari stayed guard beside him.

"How's he doing?" I asked as I handed her the last parcel of letters.

"Wakes occasionally, says some nonsense, and falls back to sleep. Nothing more," Hari said as she read over the letters. "I should have known Hackney never sent these. My aunt probably thinks I'm dead."

"I'm sorry," I whispered.

"Don't be." She placed the letter on the end table. "I should apologize to you, though."

"Huh?"

"I took my frustration with June out on you. But... that isn't fair. I want you to be safe and happy... and to be careful is all. You're like a sister to me, Leena. The last thing I want is for you to end up hurt."

"I promise I'm being careful. Really."

Hari nodded and glanced at her papers again. "Well, go get some shut-eye. We'll be in port soon."

At the mention of sleep, it was like my body realized the time. I nodded once to Hari, and with heavy footsteps, I walked out of the room.

I felt like a child waiting for a holiday; the sooner I slept, the sooner I would make a trade to change my life.

Triguá's port was unremarkable. No grand city waited for us. Dust and smoke encapsulated the hodgepodge of vendors lining the narrow street off the port. From the main deck, I scowled to myself. It looked like any other port; I might have even visited here when Mr. Hackney ran the *Sanguine Tortuga*. But when June talked about Triguá, I had pictured another miraculous port filled with magic and popery, but not every place belonged to a fairy tale. Some places belonged to nothing more than scum.

June cornered me as I left for the gangway. "C'mon, let's find Pickford."

"What? Why?"

"You're gonna need a translator if you wanna offload some of that treasure."

"Me? Here?"

"Yeah, I got some business to attend to... and we might as well try offloading some of the treasure. There's magic in these streets, and we might make a pretty penny."

"But... I don't really know how to barter."

"That's why you bring Pickford along. He'll know a good deal when he sees one. But I want you there... cause you're my first mate and all." She winked at me.

I decided not to argue and followed her. We found Pickford helping Erik in the galley as he chopped some vegetables. When June called his name, he looked up at once, hitting his head against the counter.

"Don't sneak up on me like that," Pickford grunted.

"We're offloading some of these barrels today. Are you going to help or what?" June asked.

"What's in it for me?"

"Ten percent of the profit to you personally."

"Twenty."

"Fifteen."

"Deal. As long as you pick up my brawn potion."

"Excellent." June winked at me before saying, "Unload one barrel. We don't want to lose the whole inventory. Just do your thing. You've got that bartering blood in you."

"I haven't been allowed to barter since I brought a flock of birds aboard this ship a few years ago."

"Wait, when did that happen?" I asked.

"About a year before you joined. Hackney wanted me to trade some food for gold, but they had these adorable little birds. Figured he wouldn't mind if I dropped a few birds in his office. Ha!" Pickford threw back his head with a laugh. "He was pissed. Wasn't allowed off ship for almost a year."

I could picture it happening. "Better not do that to June now."

"As long as she gets my brawn potion, I won't do anything too terrible."

"And as long as you get me a sale." June reiterated with a smile. "Now get going. We don't have all day."

If Pickford wasn't there, I would have given June a kiss goodbye. Instead, I waved to her, then followed Pickford down onto the gangway. He hoisted a barrel onto a cart, grabbed a toolbelt, and with a whistle and a pep in his step, he led me out into port.

"Y'know, we haven't spent a lot of time together since June came aboard," he said as he pushed the barrel along the ramp to port.

"We haven't?"

"Yeah, we've both been busy. I got my new place in the galley. Spending a lot of time with Erik and Kamalani. They're both sweethearts, and I'm sad I haven't gotten to know them until now. Hackney kept us doing different things... he didn't really want me baking or nothing."

"That's fantastic! The food is so much better now, too."

Pickford beamed, then continued. "And now you've got that nice setup with June. Glad she put her trust in you. Plus, I think you do her good."

"Oh... I don't know."

"You warm her."

I flushed but didn't respond, redirecting my attention to my shoes and letting Pickford lead the way. He already seemed familiar with the port, leaving me in that uncomfortably usual position of being the follower. For one moment, I flew above the sea, and everyone could look at me; I saved June, I helped her find the treasure, and I was her first mate. But now, following Pickford, I found myself back on the ground, the young, clueless girl, still learning how to spread my wings.

Pickford had seen so much; Hari showed such care; Callum had knowledge that could put leaders to shame; Theo saw more than anyone else; and June, well, she could lead. What more did I have than a flame I still couldn't control?

But June chose me for a reason, I reminded myself. She had helped unleash my power, and with it, I could only hope confidence would follow.

Or more.

"This here is probably a good spot." Pickford motioned toward a spot under a cockspur tree. "Far enough away from the main market but clear enough to draw attention. Here, help me open this barrel."

He handed me the hammer from his belt, and carefully we removed the rings around the barrel. Pickford put each ring around his arm, then pried off the lid, revealing that silver liquid.

Even now, it glistened at me with the same determination and vibrance as I found it. Every now and again, I swore I saw an image in the silver liquid: a plague doctor, a palm tree, and sometimes, a dragon. But it might have been my imagination.

If only Theo woke up, then he could tell me what this all meant!

"And now we wait," Pickford said.

"For what?"

"Customers."

"Will they come?"

"They always do. Especially here."

"Right... you've been here before."

"Yeah." Pickford removed a piece of chocolate from his upper pocket and popped it in his mouth, then said, "There aren't that many ports on the Gonvernnes continent, honestly. We often circled it regularly as a part of our trade routes. We actually came here after San Joya, but you might not have noticed. Haven't been over this way in over a year, though... Probably had to do with the map and treasure or whatever."

"I wonder why he was so fixated on it..." I ran my finger over the surface of the liquid. It bristled with excitement as if absorbing my magic and flame.

"I'm sure he had a trade charter or something. Asked Callum if he knew, but he hadn't a clue."

"No legends or anything?"

"None that Hackney shared with him. Probably didn't trust his son enough."

I chewed my inner cheek. There had to be a reason. People fought wars over magic. That much we knew to be true, but what value did Mr. Hackney have for a magical pool?

Then again, what did June?

Pickford and I said little else over the next couple of hours. A few patrons came up to our barrel and peered inside, but no one offered any trade. At one point, June walked past, nodded at us, then hurried down a dilapidated alleyway. I saw her again only after a fifth patron examined our barrel, but she didn't even stop to acknowledge us, instead hoisting a satchel over her shoulder with resolve.

What would she say if we couldn't sell this? For the most part, I was nothing more than an observer. Most customers spoke Vernnes, leaving me clueless throughout the conversation.

"Not sure how much longer we want to give this." Pickford grunted. "I guess June thought this would be a good place. This here is the perfect market for this shit."

I glanced back toward the main port. Merchants sat hunched in corners, trading vices, hiding in the shadow of authority. Magic bristled from some of their fingers, sparks flying, and prayers whistling. Their carts stood piled with obscure goods, organized in disarray. Unlike the other ports, they didn't have stalls or booths; instead, we all gathered here to sell goods without a price and barter for possibilities without limits.

"We should probably give it until sunset. Otherwise, June will have our necks." I said.

Pickford grunted but didn't argue.

We continued vending. A few more patrons came over, but other than someone offering five gold doubloons for a cup of the silver liquid, no one else came.

Until, about an hour before sunset, a man and woman approached. Their eyes caught my attention at once. The woman bore a set of mismatched green and blue eyes, while the man had the same red eyes as Theo.

"See! I told you the *Sanguine Tortuga* was here! I'd recognize that ship anywhere!" the woman exclaimed in Delinnes.

The man nodded, his red eyes fixated on the barrel.

"We told Bernard not to come back here unless he had it, so it must mean he got Huo Xiuying's map and got us the treasure, yes?"

"Huo Xiuying?"

"You'd know them as Venom Mouth," the man said.

Before I could reply, the woman pushed forward and stared into the barrel. "Yes, this is it. We have it at last. Please send our regards to Bernard."

"I'm sorry… did you have a deal with Mr. Hackney?" I asked.

"Yes, isn't that why you're here?"

"Mr. Hackney is gone. Captain Lok runs this show now," Pickford said.

"But we're willing to uphold whatever deal you had with him," I added.

"Oh?"

"Come back to the ship," I continued, letting a warm blow of confidence guide me. "I am sure our captain would love to meet you."

CHAPTER TWENTY-TWO

The Trade

Pickford led our guests to the dining hall onboard while I retrieved June.

"June!" I knocked on her door. "I've got big news! June!"

"Enter," she called.

I pushed open the door, then froze. June stood before her mirror, a strange harness in her hands. She wore only her thin undershirt over her otherwise bare chest.

My eye darted away from her at once, finding a much more interesting speck of dust on the ground.

June glanced back at me and held out the harness. "Could you help me get this on?"

"What... what is it?" I still kept my gaze away from her.

"It's the harness to affix my hook. It's more complicated than I thought."

"Oh, um, okay."

Sweat gathered in my palms as I approached her. With trembling fingers, I helped her lift the harness over her head, strapping one leather strap across her good shoulder and then across her back to the other side. Like the sleeve of a shirt, she inserted her handless arm into the contraption. At the end, a clasp with her carved seagrip hook fit perfectly onto the nub of her arm.

She turned to face me. "Help me lace the straps on my inner arm, please."

I slowly laced each strap, securing it in place along her arm. She leaned into me, only the thin layer of her under-shirt as a barrier from her skin touching me.

"Thank you," she whispered, brushing her lips against my neck, "now what was the good news?"

I'd almost forgotten why I came in here. "Right…" I straightened my back. "We found a couple of buyers."

"Oh?" She reached for her camise on the chair and dressed. "And?"

"They're on board now. They say they had a deal with Hackney for Venom Mouth's treasure. We told them we'd still honor the trade, so we invited them back so you may speak with them."

"Smart thinking." June grabbed her bodice next and put her first arm through its sleeve. At once, I raced over, helping her hooked arm into the other hole. It was almost an instinct to lace the bodice closed. How had she done this without help the past few weeks? She always looked so well put together. Why didn't she ever say she needed help?

June lifted her hook up and pressed the unsharpened edge against my cheek, then placed her other hand on my waist. She leaned in and kissed me, her lips still brushing mine as she spoke. "We'll have time to celebrate later. Let's go talk to these traders, okay?"

"Yes, Captain…" I murmured.

She smiled, kissed me one last time, then released me. Once she grabbed her jacket, I knew our alone time in the captain's quarters had ended. I followed her with a deep heat rippling through my lower body.

I pushed it back as we reached the dining hall.

Pickford had already laid out a few bowls of soup, which our guests had not bothered to touch.

June pulled one chair back and perched upon it, then said, "I apologize for the delay. I am the captain of the *Sanguine Tortuga*. How can I be of service?"

"You are the captain?" The woman asked.

"Aye."

"You cannot be over eighteen."

"Age does not matter. I have what you want. So let's make a deal."

"We made this deal initially with Mr. Hackney." The woman kept her tone level.

"Well, Bernard's dead. So I guess you're dealing with me." June did not flinch, her confidence brimming like the corona of the sun.

The woman glanced at the man, and he nodded. "Fine. What are your terms?"

"Foremost, I dislike trading without knowing a name."

The woman exhaled. "You can call me Kai. This is my husband, Nasr."

The man bowed his head.

"Kai and Nasr. Very well…" June leaned forward so her hook hit the table. "Tell me…why do you want our treasure so badly? What compelled you to make a deal with a slaver like Bernard Hackney?"

"It's obviously magic. That's valuable."

"Yes, but why *this* and not some magical flower?" June fidgeted with her pants pocket. Did she still carry the flower we stole from São Caméliosa? What was she planning to do with it?

Kai exchanged another glance with Nasr. "We knew Huo Xiuying and knew of their treasure. They were hiding it from us and those like us."

"You have yet to answer my question." June dug her hook into the table.

Nasr spoke this time, his voice low, almost a whisper, "The silver liquid… Kek's Blessing, as we call it… is one of the most powerful substances on the planet. It is the base of so many elixirs and potions, as well as the driving force of life and death. Some say… it is the lifeblood of the world."

My attention shifted to the barrel at the far end of the room. Pickford sat upon it with his arms crossed. Did we really carry something so powerful? I knew it was magic, but… the *lifeblood*? Preposterous.

"Now, why should I give it to you, though? If it is so powerful, maybe I should keep it." June kept her fascination in toe, negotiations instead mingling on the line.

"We offered Hackney a trade deal."

"Isn't that what we're doing now?"

"No, not like this. Nasr and I… we're exporters. We run a trade route here to Heims. If he found Huo Xiuying's treasure, we said we would use him as our primary supplier… not just for the magic, but for any other goods he wished to offload."

"Hence, securing his wealth for years to come?" June remarked.

"Correct."

June glanced over at Kai and Nasr. She kept her expressions blank, a true player of the game. What was she thinking now? What would she do next?

"And what is the payment?" June asked at last.

Kai closed her eyes, counting under her breath, then said, "Five thousand a barrel."

I held back the urge to scream. Five thousand doubloons?! That was more than I could ever imagine! With twelve barrels, if my math was correct, they would give us sixty-thousand doubloons!

But June played her usual game, "I want ten."

"Six," Kai replied.

"Eight."

"Seven and a half."

"Deal."

The room spun at the possibility. I never imagined quite so many riches. One barrel was worth the same amount of money my mother made in a year!

And one barrel was worth over seven of me. My mother sold me for a thousand.

She didn't even barter. She didn't even try.

I was worth less than a barrel of silver goo.

Tremors shifted through my body, and my stomach churned. Nausea mushroomed in my throat, and with a sudden lurch, I excused myself from the room. My head spun as I raced onto the main deck, found my way to the edge of the ship, and once again vomited.

I tried to avoid thinking about my mother; she did nothing more than toss me aside. But hearing them barter over these barrels brought that fateful day back to me. My mother sold me like any common good! Did she ever go looking for me? Did she even care?

How had she treated Tristan since I left? Did she treat him like a means to an end... or did she indulge him like her son?

I gripped the edge of the boat. She *sold* me into slavery. June said Mr. Hackney was a slaver, but I hadn't let the reality sink in until now.

What would my father have done? What did Tristan think? He never even got my letters!

For all he knew, I could be dead.

"Leena?"

I jumped around, "Theo!"

I hadn't expected to see Theo awake, but he stood there, frail and leaning on a cane. Dark circles hung beneath his red eyes.

"You look sad," he remarked.

"It's fine!" I ran over to hug him but hung back when he winced.

"Sorry, things hurt and..." his gaze traveled over the ship, "I'm getting my bearings still. Woke a few hours ago. Hari and Callum brought me up to speed."

"Do you know what happened to you?"

"That pool..." he blinked a few times, "it showed me... a lot at once. Too much, I guess."

"I'm just happy you're okay!" I wiped my face, swallowing down the heartbreak in my chest. "We'll have to tell Pickford and June once they're done—"

"What're they doing?"

"They are striking a deal. We brought some of the silver pool with us, and these two merchants want to set up a trade with us. We're going to be rich, Theo!"

"A... trade?"

"Yes, they said—"

"That liquid shouldn't be traded. It's a part of the earth. It can't be—I saw visions and... and... it can't be."

"What are you talking about? Mr. Hackney was going to trade it. C'mon Theo... this is everything we planned."

"If we trade it, we will burn."

"What do you mean?"

"There will be fire... and no one will escape it. Everything will burn..." his eyes lost focus, pulling him back into a trance-like state.

I didn't know what to say. It might mean nothing, but his words hung in the air.

Instead, I took his arm and said, "C'mon, let's get you back to bed. You need more rest."

I took his arm. He didn't fight it, still mumbling to himself about an inevitable flame.

I didn't return to the dining hall, instead taking a spot in the crow's nest after returning Theo to his room. Hari greeted me at the door, and once I led Theo to the bed, she and Callum returned to fawning over Theo like a child. Usually, Theo would have hated that, but in his current state, he didn't seem to care.

I didn't stay around long. Instead, I made a home in the crow's nest for the evening, watching from above as Pickford and a few others helped Kai and Nasr unload the barrels. Once ten of the twelve barrels left the ship, Nasr carried over a chest to June, which she accepted with an eager bow. She would probably spend the night in her office, counting each coin. I would join her tomorrow, perhaps, but my heart was too heavy. Theo was ill and spoke with fear, and all I could think of now was my mother and the value she placed on my life.

I leaned my head against the wall of the crow's nest and ignited the flame in my hand. The fire flickered. My father used to make the flames dance like people, but all I could do was send the flame flying. Was my magic designed for destruction?

Would he be proud of me now, aboard a ship, behaving like the pirates he swore to defeat?

Or would he toss that all aside and let me be, accepting that I'd finally found a touch of happiness?

"Leena!? You up there!?" June called.

I glanced over the edge of the crow's nest.

"Ah yeah! There you are! Come down here."

"Why don't you come up here?" I asked.

June scoffed, "I'm your captain."

"Don't play that card with me."

"Leena. Please. I want to make sure you're okay."

I grunted but didn't argue, descending the crow's nest to speak with her.

June took my hand as I hit the main deck, spinning me around once to face her. "Now, you're gonna tell me why you ran out in the middle of our biggest deal ever. Something got your head going. I'd hate for my first mate to not be her best."

I stared at the ground. "The negotiations reminded me of something."

"And that was?"

"My mother..." I sighed. "She sold me to Mr. Hackney the same way you bartered with Kai and Nasr. It... hit me while watching you talk with them. And..." I clenched my free hand, "I try not to think about it. I really do. But she... tossed me aside into this life. I don't know what I would do if I saw her again. I must live with the fact that my mother either cared more about Tristan or money than me. To her, I was disposable... and I'm scared... I'm scared that..." I let my voice trail. I couldn't say out loud what I was thinking. The last thing I wanted was to insult June.

But she inquired anyway, cupping my cheek with her good hand as she asked, "What are you scared of?"

"That... that..." A tear fell down my cheek, "That I'm disposable to you, too. What if my flame dies out or I lose another eye? I wouldn't be a very effective first mate."

"Leena Davies," June shook her head, "you are as disposable to me as the sea and the sky. I will rid you from my life the moment all the water dries and the stars no longer twinkle. And I will only let you meet your end if we find the edge of the earth, where nothing more than darkness waits. Do not worry about what your mother did to you. For I will never sell you for the life of another. This, I swear."

The urge to kiss her broke through my tears. At once, I pressed my mouth to her lips and sank into her embrace. She could carry me to the moon, and I wouldn't move.

Everyone was wrong about June. They saw a ruthless captain, but deep down, without a doubt, her heart bubbled with kindness.

She wouldn't admit it.

"C'mon now," June said as I pulled back. "Let's go count all our riches, alright?"

"I can't even imagine what fifty thousand doubloons look like," I laughed.

"You'll see." She guided me back to the captain's quarters. The heaviness in my chest finally diminished, replaced with that comforting warmth in my abdomen. I didn't want to let go of June, worried it might dissipate.

She winked at me and opened the cabin door.

And inside, more gold than I'd ever seen lay across the floor, like the sea beneath a sunrise, glowing with pride.

CHAPTER TWENTY-THREE

El Limra

L ife aboard the *Sanguine Tortuga* returned to some semblance of normalcy. We continued to sail along, stopping at ports every few days. There, June established new trading relationships while searching for tidbits of information on a variety of items: treasure, slave ships, and opportunities. I joined her at times, but some days I stayed on board the ship, rekindling my friendship with Pickford, completing my tasks, or recounting the gold still in June's quarters.

She hadn't touched a single piece of the gold from her trades, leaving it in organized piles around the room. Often, she played more with her pearl camellia than the endless piles of gold. In all honesty, I still struggled to wrap my head around it; never in my life did I imagine this many riches!

Some days at sea, June picked Callum's brain, trying to extrapolate information about his father's trade routes. Callum, despite being a well of information, only knew so much, leaving June tearing through papers left over from Mr. Hackney's reign.

I might have been the first mate, but Hari kept the ship running. She made sure everyone completed their duties while I reported details back to June. As her first mate, really, I was her confidante and friend. Perhaps that was all she ever wanted.

Life truly returned to normal when Theo returned to the crow's nest. A few days after he woke, once he ate more and rested without pain, he climbed up the ladder and took his perch without a word. It was reassuring having him up there, our constant watch guard. Now, no one could sneak up on us; we could see the world.

If he wasn't in the crow's nest, I found him down in storage, staring at the two remaining barrels of our treasure. He didn't speak when I asked him what he saw, lost in a trance, so I left him to his own devices.

And so our days continued until the day we arrived in El Limra.

June took my arm as the anchor dropped. "Leena, you're coming with me."

"Are you sure? There's a lot to do on board and—"

"Stop being a homebody. This is important."

"What is it?"

She sucked in her lips and glanced at the port before saying, "I've been poking around about your brother and mother. Wanted to see if there was any intel from people on the mainland."

"What? Why?"

"When I found those letters... realized how much you probably missed your brother and everything. Started asking questions in Triguá, but then you were so distraught over your mother. Couldn't let that slide." She shrugged, then motioned me toward the ladder. "Got some intel that I think you'll want to hear... if it's correct."

"June..." I stammered. Never did I expect her to search for my family for me. "I don't know what to say... I... thank you."

"Don't thank me yet." June stepped down the first wrung of the ladder and glanced in my direction. "Come on. Let's get a move on... we have a bit of a walk and certainly don't have all day."

June had me dress in a shawl before leaving the ship. Meanwhile, she pulled on her best suit, tucking her hair in beneath a hat. I didn't question it; some of these ports pulsed with danger, and the last thing we needed was attention drawn to us.

As soon as I got off the boat, I realized the true reason. Flyers hung around the port. My feet ached as I approached them.

A sketch of a girl with an eyepatch stared back at me.

I stared back at me.

It was a poor drawing, but I knew it was me.

"They started popping up a few ports ago. Came from São Caméliosa. Got a good look at you but not at me, I guess." June said.

I didn't reply.

"Good thing you're not wearing that eyepatch, huh?"

I touched the scar over my eye. Since our encounter with the seagrip, I hadn't put the eyepatch back on my face, wearing my scar without flinching. "Yeah," I whispered, "guess so."

June placed a hand on my arm. "Keep your head down and your fire in toe, okay?"

I still didn't speak. My attention remained locked on the flyer. Not at the picture. Not at the description.

But at the price.

The authorities of Gonvernnes offered seven thousand doubloons for my arrest.

I was worth more as a criminal than as my mother's daughter.

Would June trade me for a chance at that bounty? The doubt weaseled its way into my stomach. What if she was taking me there now? I'd convinced myself she wouldn't harm me… but what if everyone was right? What if I was nothing more than a means to another handful of riches?

"Seven thousand…" June laughed to herself. "That's a cheap price. You're worth far more than that."

"Then what price do you place on me?" I asked.

June pressed her finger to my bottom lip and traced it. "Even if I had a number, it wouldn't be enough."

My nerves settled, and I held June in my gaze for a moment before releasing her with a nod.

We hurried along the road and away from port. Already, our crew was out in the streets. Hari and Callum walked along, talking with the shopkeepers, heads together. Pickford perused the different food vendors. And even Theo left his perch on the ship, pacing with his hands in his pockets as he looked over the different tables. He smiled woefully in my direction as I passed. Ever since he woke up, there'd been a switch in his behavior. He didn't invite me into the crow's nest to watch the stars, and at dinner, he hardly touched his meal. I still strained to fathom what he saw in our silver treasure, but perhaps I never would understand.

As June promised, the trek to our destination took time. My feet ached as we marched over the uneven roads, looping through towering structures, abandoning the façade of wealth by the port. As we walked, the occasional gasp of early autumn winds bellowed down the street like a tunnel, pushing back as we climbed uphill.

While my exhaustion increased, excitement rose like nausea in my throat. What information had June found out? Was Tristan here? Did he leave Janis to see the world? If it were him, what would I say? What would I do? My mind raced. Would I even recognize him? He had been such a scrawny kid. If my flame ignited me, what did his fire do?

The questions raced around my brain, only for June to pull me out with a tug of the sleeve.

"We're almost there," she said. We had entered a residential part of the city, lined with communal homes. A tavern and a shop snuck their way between the buildings. Garbage loitered in the road, intermingling with the few homeless individuals begging on the corners.

"Where is there?" I asked her.

"To where you'll get the truth."

"Yes, but… who are we seeing?"

June didn't answer.

"June…"

She sighed and slowed down in front of one of the tenement halls. Without looking at me, she said, "On the third floor of this building, in the fifth room to the left, in room twenty-two, you'll find a woman who you know. She will have your answers."

"A woman… I know…" I turned to the door. The rusted number "22" sat on the doorframe. "My mother is here?"

June only said, "I'll wait down here."

I don't know how long I waited to open the door. Each step toward it felt like a mile, and even as my fingers touched the doorknob, the brass weighed like a thousand ships. The door creaked open, shrieking like the wind.

And with each step, my body swayed like the waves.

What was my mother doing here? What about Tristan? What had she done?

My fire rose within my stomach as I approached the third floor. It took all my focus to keep them away from my fingertips and maintain my composure. I could not show anger. I could not show fear. That would only cause my mother to win.

On the third floor, the fifth door waited for me with its peeled exterior. Why had my mother traded her life on Janis for this room? In this house? In this port?

Why?

With a knock, I waited for my answers.

But no one came to the door.

I knocked again.

Nothing.

Was she not home?

I tried one more time.

"Hold on! Sheesh! Let me get dressed!" I knew that voice. It was the one that yelled at me to behave, the one that told me to sit in a corner, and the one that sold me like any common trade.

I didn't speak. If I spoke, I might lose myself to frustration and tears.

No, I would reel it in close to my heart; I would not crumble at my mother's feet.

My heart twisted as the door opened.

As I expected, my mother stood in the doorway of a dusty single room, peeling with paint and dust. I might not have recognized her at first. Her dark hair had turned gray, her skin was jaundiced, and her nails appeared yellow and unevenly cut. She looked me over with bloodshot eyes and licked her chapped lips. There was no excitement, no joy, only mild shock written on her face as she said my name.

"Leena."

"Mother."

We stared at each other, waiting for the other to speak. Neither of us approached. Waiting.

Our emotions boiling.

And the building creaking.

My mother broke the silence. "I see you stopped wearing your eye patch."

I touched the scar on my face. There was no reason to hide. Not anymore.

"Is that a problem?" I asked.

She shrugged and turned away from me. "Why are you here, Leena?"

I stepped forward, my nerves shaking with the rage carved into my soul. "Why am I here? That's what you have to say after you haven't seen me in years!?"

My mother still didn't face me. "Why should I be excited to see you? You're a criminal."

"I'm not—"

"Your face is plastered throughout the city."

"That might be anyone," I seethed.

"No. I know my daughter. I always knew you were trouble." She spoke without flinching as if she had rehearsed these statements for years. Had she been playing out all the possible outcomes of my arrival? Had she been dreading the day I knocked on her door?

I tried to keep the same composure, but with each passing moment, my fire grew. "I am what *you* made me."

"How many times did I ask you to behave?"

"I was a child."

"You caused your father's death."

The heat grew in the center of my palms. I clenched my fist tight, tapering the flame. "I was a child who stayed out late one night. My father protected me."

"Yes, but how many times did I tell you not to leave at night? How many times did you ignore me?"

I shook my head. "Is that what this was all about, then? Father's death? You don't think that has haunted me every day since?! Is this why you *sold* me?"

"I did not sell you." My mother spun to face me again. Her eyes burned with anger. "I gave you a chance to see the world!"

"You exchanged money for me to go with Mr. Hackney. You *sold* me."

"I gave you freedom."

"Freedom?" I scoffed. How dare she think she gave me freedom! That was something I told myself as a child, but she should have known better.

She was my mother.

Her job was to love me and to protect me. Not sell me for less than a barrel of water.

"Life on the *Sanguine Tortuga* was anything but *free*," I hissed. "I was trapped, left to the devices of a man with a hunger for power. Even if I got to travel and see the world, that is not *freedom*. I did not have a say in my future. *You* bartered it away for me."

"Don't be selfish. Didn't you want me to save your brother?" My mother changed her tune again. Every word I spoke became a pawn in her game. I just wanted the truth!

"If you saved Tristan, then where is he now?" I asked.

She could have lied. How would I have known if she said he was married? Or if he joined the navy? Or something else entirely? But, with that question, her eyes grew distant. She opened her mouth to speak a couple times but gave up, sinking back into her grimy room and reaching for the door.

I stopped it from closing with my foot.

"You didn't pay his bail, did you?" I asked.

"No! Of course I did. He's... he didn't come with me here. He stayed on Janis—"

"You're lying." I kicked the door open with my knee. "You did not free Tristan. You left Janis, didn't you? And for what? To live in this disgusting tenement hall alone? What did that accomplish?"

"Leena... you don't understand..."

"What is there to understand!? You sold me, took the money, and left my brother to rot in prison! What sort of mother does that?"

She stammered. A more cunning woman would have woven a lie; a stronger woman would have told me the truth without flinching; a wiser woman would have known this day might come. My mother was none of these things. I saw it now; she did not have Hari's compassion, Theo's insight, Pickford's friendship, Callum's knowledge, or June's loyalty. She was nothing.

Only a greedy, heartless woman who chose her own happiness over her children.

I released the door, "Goodbye, Mother. Thank you for everything."

My mother stood there, staring at me, still at a loss for words. Did she think I'd come crawling back to her? Did she think I'd still be her weak adolescent daughter?

No. Never again.

No one could control me.

Just like the fire raging in my soul.

I started to turn, then stopped. My flame bubbled beneath the surface, riding on the coattails of my anger. It begged to be set free.

My hand unclenched. In my palm, warmth grew.

Then I raised my hand...

And set the room ablaze with a single gasp.

And a scream from my mother.

I didn't say a word to June as I walked back to the ship. In my mind, I replayed the image of my mother, surrounded by my flame in the tenement. Part of me mourned whatever bond I burned. But the other part of me breathed a sigh of relief. She stole my life, so I would leave her with the scars.

Even as we returned to port and familiar faces greeted us, I did not speak. Hari tried to corner me about the wanted flyers, but I shrugged it off with a wave of my hand. I had no time for her or even for Pickford's offering of chocolate ganache as I boarded the ship and stomped past the galley. On my way up, I stole a bottle of rum from the cupboard.

Instead, my feet carried me to the empty crow's nest, away from everyone. Up there, I could breathe, alone with my thoughts. Perhaps later, Theo might join me and help me sort through the events.

If my mother survived my flame, she would go through life with her freedom stolen.

Just as she had sold my freedom for almost nothing at all.

If she died, well... then at least she died knowing what she created.

I drank alone, watching as the sky turned red over El Limra. What sort of mother would sell her daughter and let her son rot in jail? How did she rationalize it?

Did I even want to know?

The rum went down as bitter as my emotions.

How dare she!

"Leena!?" June called.

I didn't budge.

"Leena! Get down here! I wanna talk to you."

I still didn't move. If she wanted to talk so badly to me, she could climb up the ladder herself.

"Leena…" she grunted, her obvious pacing around the crow's nest echoing beneath me. A breathy curse escaped her lips.

Then the movement of her climbing up the ladder followed.

By the time she entered the crow's nest, her face had turned pale, sweat padding her forehead. She closed her eyes as she found a place to sit, murmuring a few times before settling down against the half wall of the crow's nest.

"You really made me climb all the way up here…" She exhaled on the last word.

I watched as she gripped the ground, still refusing to open her eyes.

"Are you scared of heights?" I asked.

June didn't speak, clenching her jaw tight.

"You are, aren't you?!"

"What does it matter?" June whispered and forced one eye open to look at me. "I am here now."

"Was it so important that you had to climb up here to bother me?" I asked.

She grabbed my bottle of rum and took a long drink before saying, "You're distressed. I was worried."

"I need time to process what happened. That is all."

"Well, we're changing course and heading to Janis."

"What?"

She put down the bottle and looked across at me. "Janis is a good trade partner. It would be wise for us to establish connections. Some of our crew members have connections there too…" She eyed me, each word chosen with care. "It would be smart to utilize them."

"June…"

"That is all I wanted to tell you," she gulped and glanced back at the ladder, "I'll leave you now."

"June, wait!" I grabbed her hand and pulled her toward me. Tears prickled my eye. Of course, I knew what she meant by this. And I couldn't hold back my excitement. So I kissed her hard on the lips, her mouth deeply entwined with mine. As I pulled away, I could only murmur, "Thank you."

She replied by returning the kiss. This time, she moved with tenderness, with one hand resting over my waist. I moved closer to her, our bodies touching. In that moment, I wanted nothing more than for her to pull me into her embrace and let me explore every inch of her skin.

I brought my mouth to her neck and moved down it, tasting her sweat and inhaling her like the ocean. Her fingers moved up, pulling the warmth in my core out like a puppet master and her strings.

"You are worth more than a thousand doubloons," June murmured into my skin. "Remember that."

"Because of my flame?" I asked, my breath trampling over my words.

"Because of everything." June unlaced the first eyelet of my bodice. "And I will go down with this ship before I betray you. This, I swear."

I kissed her again as her fingers danced to the next eyelet. As she unlaced it, I kicked off my shoes and hurled them over the edge of the crow's nest.

Where they stayed until the sun rose the next morning.

CHAPTER TWENTY-FOUR

The Ship in the Mist

T he next morning I woke with June's coat draped over me and shoes still lost beneath the crow's nest. June had long left me, but the lingering truths we shared in our most vulnerable hours remained. In those short moments, I learned more about June than I ever thought possible. And I could recite the story now like the back of my hand.

"The *Basil Weasel* took me from my home in Sīchóu Shíyóu when I was a little girl," she whispered, lying beside me, running her hand through my hair. "At the time, my name was Lu Jun, but the captain of that ship kept calling me June Lok... so that became the name I claimed. I never went back to the name Lu Jun. For years, that was all I knew... until Venom Mouth slaughtered the crew and took me on board. Those years I was free... I learned all of this..." she waved her hand around us. "They were a bad person, but... they taught me to live."

"There are no good people," I replied, leaning against her shoulder. When I closed my eye, I still saw my mother burning in room twenty-two.

"Some are better than others," June said, then pulled me into another devouring kiss.

Later that same evening, I pried more, and her answer to my question still hung in the air as I sat in the crow's nest.

"Why are you scared of heights?" I had asked.

She didn't reply at first, gazing through me to some distant memory.

"You don't have to tell me."

But she did. "On board the *Cobalt Hare*, I had a friend. Bobbie. We were... close." She blinked once, then smirked at me. "He and I came aboard the *Cobalt Hare* around the same time. We loved to cause trouble for Freda. But while I had a way to keep myself from harm, claiming to be Venom Mouth's daughter and all, he didn't. One day, he snuck into Freda's liquor stash. Seemed innocent enough, but she was livid. Freda chased him up the crow's nest... and... pushed him."

She didn't need to say more.

And I didn't ask.

In the crow's nest, all our walls dropped.

But even after I picked my shoes off the ground the next morning, those walls didn't return. June sat perched on one of the nearby boxes. When she smiled at me, it held no hidden agenda.

Only her. My dear friend.

The woman I'd follow to the edge of the earth.

And the walls stayed crumbled as each day passed. Between intermittent summer storms and rocking waves, I always found a way back into June's arms by the end of the night. She didn't dare venture into the crow's nest again, but we didn't need some perch above the rest of the ship to open our souls.

Everything, really, felt right.

Hari served as quartermaster, issuing orders and keeping the ship running. Pickford continued his experimentation in the galley with Erik and Kamalani, serving new fish pies and sweet desserts. Theo resumed his perch when the crow's nest was free, staring out at sea. And even Callum, usually quiet and uninvolved, approached June one day with a red flag. On it, he painted a skeletal tortoise—our very own sanguine tortuga.

June removed the old worn-down flag, its image tattered and forgotten, and hoisted it up above the crow's nest. She smiled wider than I'd ever seen. The grin was contagious, and that evening, with Pickford on his harmonica, we danced and sang.

At least until a gentle rain grabbed hold of the sky.

June's cabin became my new home, and even as the rain fell, I disappeared with her into the captain's quarters. As I sat on the chair in the corner of her bedroom and wrung out my hair, June approached, holding something close in her hand.

"I want you to have something." She opened her palm.

Inside, the crystalized flower we stole from São Caméliosa twinkled at me. It had decreased in size but still shimmered with its distant whisper of magic. June had attached a chain to it as well.

"I don't have a use for it anymore," she continued. "You should have it. You are the reason we found it."

"Why's it smaller?" I asked.

"The petals... I used them to get information..." She stroked the outside of the flower. "They're worth quite a bit... and people will give up a lot for them. All because they're magic."

"Magic is valuable..."

Her eyes glimmered in my direction. "But only if someone knows how to use it."

"You think I know how to use my magic?"

"Enough to not burn me."

I took the flower from her. She had woven it onto a chain, a simple necklace made for a queen. "Don't you want to use it still?"

"Nah, I got the information I need with it. Besides…" She placed it around my neck. "It was always your flower to begin with."

I stared at it. "You used it to get information about my mother, didn't you?"

"Mhm." She helped me put the necklace around my neck. As she clasped it closed, she kissed the spot between my shoulder blades.

And with her fingers on my skin, I sank into her touch.

My captain.

And in those moments, I was her queen.

I woke entangled in June's arms, but not to the sunrise like most days. Rather, to the ringing of the bell on deck.

"What the—" I rubbed my eye. "What's going on?"

"Don't have a clue, but whoever is ringing that bell is dead…" June grunted as she climbed out of bed. She picked a nightgown off the floor and threw it at me, then pulled on her own nightshirt. Once dressed, I helped her equip her hook, and together we left the room as the bell continued its toll.

Pickford stood by the bell, still ringing it with a grin on his face. The rest of the crew had already climbed on deck, gathered around Pickford with scowls. Hari leaned into Callum, her attention half on Pickford, fingers wrapped around Callum's arm. I half smiled to myself at the scene; perhaps, despite everything, on our little pirate ship... we were never meant to be anywhere else.

"There better be a goddamn seagrip out there." June snapped.

The ringing stopped, and Pickford turned to June. "Dunno. Theo asked me to ring it."

"What does he want now?"

"There's something out there," Theo called from the crow's nest. With ease, he descended the ladder, joining us on deck. The lantern light caused his red eyes to flare. Beneath it, he looked older, worn down by his comatose state those weeks ago. Part of me felt bad; he and I had spent little time together since he woke, hiding in the crow's nest most days.

"And it warranted waking us up?" June kept her gaze tight on Theo.

"I think it's one of the *Commeant*'s ships."

June's face hardened. "Which one?"

"Can't tell."

June approached the edge of the deck, staring out at the mist-riddled sea. I squinted my one good eye but couldn't see anything.

"It's beyond the mist... in the Vapor Pit." Theo stepped toward the railing. "Can you see it?"

"Not at all." June continued staring. "Are you positive it's just one ship?"

"Yes. Small vessel. Half our size, at least."

"It might be the *Basil Weasel* or the *Amber Mouse*," June remarked.

Theo instead replied, "I can't tell. The mist in the Vapor Pit makes my sight murky."

June didn't move, her attention locked on the water. She tightened her hand around the railing, her knuckles white.

"June, I know what you're thinking," Hari said. "But take a moment to consider our options."

At first, June didn't reply, her gaze still locked on the water. Her response arrived as a whisper. "You know why they locked me up on the *Cobalt Hare*? It was because I almost freed that crew. Hackney didn't expect it... so I succeeded here... but it doesn't mean there aren't countless more *Commeant* ships stealing children from their homes."

"It's not our job to save them. It could be a trap or a fishing boat or—"

"Venom Mouth didn't hesitate to attack." She turned to face Hari. "If you want to sit idly by, fine. But I ask everyone on this crew: did you not dare to act until someone came with a beacon in hand? Did you ever think you'd find hope again? We are the hope for the people on *that* ship. And I hope some of you will join me in this cause."

No one spoke. Even Hari's head fell.

I joined June's side and glanced at Theo. "Is it definitely a small ship?"

Theo nodded slowly.

"And it's definitely a part of the *Commeant*?"

Another slow nod.

"Then I'm sure we can take it." I turned back to June. "I am with you."

"Would hope so," she said.

"Eh, if Leena's in, then why not? Sure, let's do it." Pickford added.

One by one, the crew murmured their agreement. We weren't the same group of exhausted pirates who denied June the attack months ago. We'd defeated a seagrip, we found a priceless treasure, and we could run this ship like any other crew at sea.

And we would go down with our captain and our ship.

Well, at least I would.

Essie navigated the *Sanguine Tortuga* slowly through the mist. While Hari bellowed orders to hoist the sails, June bounded between each position, checking in with each member of the crew. She kept reaching for the daggers on her hips, then relaxing. From my perch in the crow's nest, I watched her anxious waltz. This was the first time she would truly live up to Venom Mouth's name. While Venom Mouth still left a sting in my heart and a haunting memory in my soul, I knew June saw that pirate as a hero.

But I still didn't know why they killed my father. What had he done? If they were trying to free slaves, then why kill my father?

Why burn out my eye?

The mist gobbled us whole as we sailed forward, inching beneath the half-moon light. A light drizzle danced on my skin.

"We haven't been up here together in a while..." Theo said, his eyes steady.

"Yeah. It's kind of nice being up here again." I followed his gaze but still saw nothing.

"I just..." Theo inhaled once, "I want you to know that... none of this was because of you."

"What?"

He blinked a couple of times. "On the island, I mean. When I reacted to the silver pool. It wasn't because of you."

"Oh. Okay. Thank you." I picked at my nail, still focused on the sea. Why would Theo mention that? Why now?

I'd ask later. For now, my attention remained on the horizon, searching for a ship with my faulty vision. A weird mix of excitement and fear danced on my skin. Would the people we rescue join our crew? Would we now have a second ship? I was sure June had a plan with the way she marched about, scanning the horizon.

And everyone waited, adjusting the sails, tracking the sea.

Would we be able to do this? Or was this just another dream, led forward by our captain with a vendetta?

So we would wait.

We would hope.

We would dream.

And we would act.

"She's off our starboard side," Theo's shouts broke the silence.

I pulled away, racing to the other side of the crow's nest. June had already reached the starboard side, focused on the water.

At first, I didn't see the ship.

The smoke of the Vapor Pit wavered, capturing the moment like a gasp of air.

And out of it emerged a ship. Not a small ship.

But a familiar one.

June knew it too. She instantly shot a glare up at the crow's nest. "Theo!"

But he wasn't paying any attention. His own gaze had returned to the water, where an orange glow encapsulated the edge of the approaching ship.

And a roaring flame exploded off the main deck of the *Cobalt Hare*.

CHAPTER TWENTY-FIVE

The Pyromancer

T he fire swelled on the decks of the *Cobalt Hare*, and before I blinked, it raced toward the *Sanguine Tortuga*. I opened my arms, willing the fire into my grasp. It raced forward like the seagrip and ensconced me, like the way lightning chases after the tallest tree. But the fire did not burn. With a single gasp, I took away its life. It reduced to embers on the floor of the crow's nest, leaving behind only a thick plume of smoke as a mask.

"Leena!" Hari's voice rang out.

"They're attacking! Get to your stations." I caught a new flame in my hand, eyeing the *Cobalt Hare* from across the water through the smoke. Confidence welled in my throat. How dare they attack me with *my* element!

"Theo, what type of weaponry are we dealing with?" I asked my friend.

He continued to stare, unmoving.

"Theo!"

He still didn't say a word.

I tore my attention away, focusing on the ship. With the wind bellowing in its sails, it moved toward us with determination. Hari readied her harpoon at the helm while others prepared their weapons with fear. The *Cobalt Hare* stood taller, prouder, and with more artillery. How would we be able to fight it? Even with my flame, I could only do so much.

"Leena! What do you want us to do?" Pickford called.

"Why are you asking me?"

"You're the first mate!"

"But June's the captain!"

"Yeah, then where is she!?" Pickford barked.

My shoulders fell. "Wasn't she right there?"

"No, she's gone!"

I cursed, scanning the deck.

Theo answered Pickford, his voice almost a whisper, caught by the wind and the sea. "She's turning herself in…"

"What!?"

"See…" Theo pointed at the water. A small rowboat had already escaped off our starboard side, heading toward the *Cobalt Hare*, using the smoke of the vapor pit as a disguise.

"Dammit, June!" I clung to the railing. This was exactly what I would expect from her.

The first time, I stopped her.

The second time, she saved me.

This time… I would join her.

"Hari!" I shouted as I descended the crow's nest. "Raise the defenses and move the ship back! I'm going to get our foolish captain!"

Hari obeyed at once, falling into step with her role. I still wondered why June didn't make her first mate; she had so much more skill in this. I was just June's… lover? Partner?

I never labeled what we were, but I guess it didn't matter.

"Leena, wait!" Pickford caught my arm. "You're gonna need some muscle. Let me help."

"No, stay here. I want you safe. Besides, the ship needs a chef."

"I'm not the chef."

"You might as well be. I've watched with Erik and Kamalani in the kitchen. You're fantastic."

Pickford released my arm, sadness reflective in his face, lips curled in a frown. "Be safe."

"And you best come back!" Hari shouted from her harpoon gun. "I don't want to be in charge of this ship."

"Aye!" I replied, then with a last difficult smile, I rushed over to the jolly boats off the side of the ship. Questions rotated in my head as I raised the boat to my level. But my heart focused solely on June as she distanced herself from the *Sanguine Tortuga* and approached the *Cobalt Hare*.

As I climbed into the boat, to my surprise, Callum raced over to me. He held a spyglass in his hands. Fear turned his already pasty skin as white as a sheet.

"Leena! Wait!"

"Callum, I have to go get June—"

"They have a pyromancer!" He interrupted me.

"What?"

"I imagine Theo saw… but I can't think why he didn't tell you. But I was looking, and that flame came from a person, not a weapon." He wiggled the spyglass in his hand. "The *Cobalt Hare* is basically the same as our ship. We don't have any cannons or weapons that can produce that sort of fire. To install something like that would take *years*."

"Are you sure they don't have one?"

"I went aboard the *Cobalt Hare* with my father those months ago when they were making a deal for June. They didn't have any fire-producing artillery."

"But are you sure it was a pyromancer?"

"I was looking at the ship when they attacked. The fire came from a person. Theo should have seen it." Callum glanced at the crow's nest.

I followed his gaze. Why hadn't Theo told me? Did the silver pool affect his sight?

But he also led us here, facing the *Cobalt Hare* with our minuscule crew.

My voice quivered as I spoke the next words, "Put Theo in the brig. I'm going to get June."

Never did I consider myself a good paddler, but I maneuvered the rowboat with all my might as I hurried after June. I lost track of her, weaving in and out of the smoke. The *Cobalt Hare* didn't react, either. Did they even see her? If not, then I might just have enough time to stop her.

Theo kept appearing in my mind. When I told Callum to send him to the brig and then passed the message along to the rest of the crew, there was a despondent acceptance. Theo still waited in the crow's nest, watching, as if he knew what was to come.

Why did he bring us here?

This could be it, the end of our freedom.

Didn't he care?

My shoulders screamed as I continued paddling. Each ache tore at my muscles. The haze made my already limited vision worse, but I did not falter.

"June!" I cried, but the wind caught my voice and threw it behind me.

I kept on forward, shifting in and out of the mist, growing closer to the *Cobalt Hare*. If I could feel my arms after this, it would be a miracle, but I would not let my captain go down alone.

I would not let my friend leave me.

As I neared the *Cobalt Hare*, another burst of light filled my vision. Once again, a fireball mounted off the edge of the ship, spiraling back toward the *Sanguine Tortuga* in the distance. This fireball moved like a seagrip, maneuvering through the sky in a gasp of smoke. If I had a moment to marvel at its artistry, I would have paused; instead, I dropped my paddle and extended my hand. Sweat bubbled on my forehead. The fire would not harm the ship.

I wouldn't let it.

It all happened so fast. As the thoughts fled through my mind, I willed the flame to me. It twisted around in the sky before slithering down into the water. It skidded over the surface, heading straight for my boat.

With my hands outstretched, I ordered it to disintegrate.

But this time, the flame did not diminish but ventured onto my boat.

And me.

The flame engulfed me.

My skin did not burn.

But my boat did.

I pushed along the water at my swiftest speed, the *Cobalt Hare* so close now that I saw the barnacles dangling from its wood.

And as the fire flared around me, there I saw her. June had parked her boat along the rear side of the ship near one of the porthole windows. She had already thrown a rope into the window, and with her hook as a stabilization tool, she began her ascent. I wanted to call to her, but I kept my voice to myself. She moved with agile grace; I still didn't know how she mastered her special hand with such precision. And as she squeezed herself through the porthole window, I couldn't help but marvel at her skill.

And with my attention stolen, the *Cobalt Hare* acted.

Another bellow of fire escaped from the ship.

Before I turned, the fire surrounded me.

And sent me flying into the water like a fiery gust from a hurricane.

A fishing net saved me.

As I floundered in the water, it fell from the main deck and hoisted me aboard, treating me as nothing more than a simple fish in the water.

I struggled against the netting, each gasp in tune with the creaking of the levy pulling me aboard the ship. From above, I watched as my rowboat disappeared into embers. Nothing more than the waste of the sea.

A crewmate hoisted the net onto the deck. They tossed me to the side, where I lay there, gasping for breath. A set of pristine boots greeted me.

Owned by a familiar face.

"You're not June Lok." Captain Freda Platt snarled down at me.

"I'm not." I gripped the damp rungs of the net.

"Who are you?"

She didn't remember. Back then, I was nothing more than Hackney's useless acquiree.

Now, I was so much more.

My flame pulsed in my hands, drying the water around me. I replied carefully, "I'm nobody."

"Typical response." Freda scoffed. "Bring her to the brig. I don't have time for this."

As the crewmates cut open the ropes, I acted.

The ocean could not taper my flame; it was there, I found it in my heart to act.

So I let it erupt from me in a storm meant for the clouds.

The fire laced around the crewmate. With the smoke as my new shield, I ran across the deck, letting the fire follow me. It was like being on board the *Sanguine Tortuga*, really. Everything was bigger but sat in the same place; I navigated it like the back of my hand.

"Davies!" Freda cried after me.

I guess she did know my name. What a liar.

My heart fixated on June as I ducked beneath the deck. While my fire roared on deck, I reduced it to flickering sparks as I hurried forward. Wherever she was, we would fight together.

For better or worse.

I slowed my pace, weaving beneath crates and barrels, hiding in the same places I knew on board the *Sanguine Tortuga*. The darkness tempted me to use my flame, but I stayed in the shadows. Waiting…

Listening…

What if they found me? What if I came face-to-face with their pyromancer? How long could I fight them? I was nothing more than a rogue performer.

I remained still.

Listening…

Waiting…

Floorboards creaked.

Then a shadow, masked by a glow of orange, entered my peripheral. I didn't dare turn, waiting as the figure came into view. They moved, slowly and carefully, through the boxes. I held my breath, keeping my fire in tow.

Instead, the figure came with a fire in the palm of their hand. A lifeless twinkle haunted the crewmate's eyes.

While the fire basked in the fury of their orange hair.

As I caught a glimpse of their face, my entire body froze. It'd been years, but I knew it was him.

Despite my instincts, I rose to my feet.

"Tristan?" I choked. "Is that you?"

CHAPTER TWENTY-SIX

Battle of the Cobalt Hare

T ristan stared at me. He opened his mouth to speak, but nothing came out. In the dim orange light, I recognized his long jaw and nose. Freckles covered his face while his greasy orange hair lay swept to the side. He'd gained muscle since I last saw him all those years ago. In so many ways, he even looked like our father, except for his clear inability to grow a full beard.

"How do you know me?" Tristan spoke, voice low. The fire continued in his palms.

"It's me. It's Leena. Your sister. See," I stepped into the light so he could see the scar on my face.

"My sister is dead," he stated, but his face twisted with uncertainty. "June Lok killed her."

"No. It's me. Tristan—"

"Liar!" He sent a flame in my direction.

I caught it with one swoop and let it diminish. Despite my racing heart, I kept my voice level. "When we were children, we used to go out with our father on the pier and watch the dolphins. One time, you jumped in the water, and before our father could save you, the dolphin picked you up on its back. You rode around on it for an hour, and when you got back to the shore, I was excited to ride it, but it vanished. I was jealous for a week!"

Tristan lowered his hand, but the flame did not go out.

I found another story. "After our father passed away, you and I used to spend hours on the beach building sandcastles in our father's name. We weren't very good, but we built a fortress so tall that some of the barking penguins made it their home. You named the male penguin Mister Beaker."

Tears filled my eye as I spoke, keeping my gaze level with Tristan. He remained in defense, but his bottom lip had begun to quiver.

I kept going, "When we were fourteen, my mother sold me to the *Commeant* in order to pay your bail. I joined the crew of the *Sanguine Tortuga*, yearning for the day I would return to you. But our mother didn't pay your bail, and she left me as a slave on a ship. I've spent years wanting to find you again, Tristan. Please... believe it's me. Please."

The fire reduced to embers on his fingertips. "Leena..."

I simpered.

He analyzed me. "You have fire too? That was you?"

"I guess Dad gave it to both of us."

He opened his mouth to respond, but a shadow moved behind him. A hand emerged from the shadows, a knife in hand, and pressed against his throat.

"June!" I hissed. "Stop! That's my brother!"

I raised my hand so that my fire lit the room. June stood there, her knife extended, holding Tristan in place. Fear did not cross his eyes, and he kept his position firm, like a loyal soldier.

"Is it?" She asked, stealing a glance between the two of us. "Ah yeah, I see the family resemblance."

Tristan said nothing.

"Well... if you're Leena's brother... then take me to Freda." June hissed in his ear.

"And why should I do that?" He asked.

"I need to talk to her."

"June, we should go," I whispered, "We're outnumbered and—"

"No. I have to do this."

"Why?"

"You know why."

I did. Of course I did. But I didn't have to like it.

"So, Mr. Davies," June kept her knife against my brother's throat, "will you take me to your captain?"

"Yes. I can."

Tristan suddenly lunged backward into June's body, sending a wave of fire in my direction. I jumped back, shouting and catching the fire before it burned the surrounding boxes. Smoke filled the hallway, and when it cleared, Tristan and June had vanished.

I cursed, then bounded after them. As I ran, I nearly tripped on three separate bodies dripping with blood. This time, my heart didn't quiver at their sight. All those months ago, when I first escaped Mr. Hackney's grasp, June's actions sent fear down my spine. Now I saw the truth behind each slaughter. These were *her* slavers; these were the people who took *her* freedom after Venom Mouth's death.

She saved me from Mr. Hackney. I would do the same for her.

As I reached the ladder to head back on deck, I paused. The clanking of swords echoed from above, a chorus of shouts joining in the instrumental ringing. There was something compelling about the musical intonations of battle. Pickford used to tell us stories of sirens and how they would lock you in their song. Perhaps the true siren was the war waged at sea and the screams that followed as we attacked.

So hearing this song, it did not come as a surprise as I climbed the ladder to find my crew from the *Sanguine Tortuga* on deck, attacking the *Cobalt Hare*. The *Sanguine Tortuga* itself parked itself along the hull, its red flag casting a shadow over the deck. My crew moved with dexterity. I caught glimpses of a few as I rushed forward into the commotion. Pickford moved with ease amongst the crew, wielding two cutlasses with precision. I'd never seen him move like that, but each step came with ease. Erik threw barrels, causing a crewmate of the *Cobalt Hare* to go flying into the water. Hari worked magic with the harpoon gun from the deck of the *Sanguine Tortuga*. Even Callum took part in the commotion, a slim knife in hand, darting between the crewmates.

Everyone fought. The crew. June's crew.

My crew.

We would not let the *Cobalt Hare* take us. Any of us.

I raced into the battle with fire on my hands. Using the fire as a shield, I searched in the commotion for Tristan and June. I couldn't find it in my heart to blame Tristan for taking June; however, he ended up on the *Cobalt Hare*. He acquired the same distaste as his captain. I would have as well. I only hoped they hadn't killed each other. June would, given the chance, but I had only just found my brother. I couldn't lose him again.

As the battle waged on, I continued to control my fire, using it to distract different crew mates while searching crowd. But the crowd only continued to grow, unfamiliar faces joining the battle.

Were these the acquirees of the *Cobalt Hare*? Was that why June ventured aboard on her own? Did she rally these troops as she did aboard the *Sanguine Tortuga*?

A scream pulled my attention as I slashed a crewmate's face with fire.

"CALLUM!" Hari's shriek pierced the air.

A large figure stood over Callum's body in a corner. A bloodied sword hung from the figure's hand. Pale and decrepit, Callum's body twitched but his eyes did not move. Red blanketed his skin. I caught Hari's worry instantly, and without hesitating, I raced over to the crewmate with my fire roaring.

As he turned, I sliced the fire across his face. The crewmate stumbled backward, hitting the railing.

Before he could fall over, the spear from the harpoon gun pierced his back, and he fell forward in a pool of his own blood.

I didn't watch him die. My attention instantly went back to Callum's body.

Only for Tristan to step in front of me.

"Leena, leave!" He commanded, just like he did when we were kids.

"This is my crew and my battle."

"You'll get hurt. Please. Just get below deck, and you and I can escape and—"

I interrupted him. "Where's June?"

He kept on his own tirade. "We can go back to Janis and be safe. I'm sure that Gov—"

"Tristan! Where is June!?"

"What does it matter!? She's your captor!"

"No! She's my captain!"

"Leena…"

"I helped her take the *Sanguine Tortuga*. This is my crew!" I motioned to the *Sanguine Tortuga*. "I'm her first mate."

"You're—"

"Tristan! Mr. Hackney was my slaver. Mother SOLD me to him. June helped set me free… which is what she is trying to do here to you! Please! Where is she!?"

Tristan's attention fell to the floor, still processing everything I said. I didn't have time for him to think. I needed answers.

"Dammit, Tristan! Tell me!"

Without a word, he pointed to the *Cobalt Hare*'s crow's nest.

My stomach lurched. Freda and June stood, embattled, on the top of the ship. Each of June's steps, swift and in motion, came with a sort of fear that I knew ached deep in her bones. If she kept being distracted, I knew it would not end well.

I didn't wait for Tristan to say anything else. Instead, I rushed through the crowd, sending waves of fire as my defense, and hurried up the ladder to the crow's nest. As I climbed, I burned the ladder, preventing anyone from stopping me. My heart cried for June, begged for her to be safe.

Clunking sent fear up my spine. Each clank of the sword, each thud of a footstep, meant one step closer to death. June just had to hold on a bit longer.

Just a bit longer—

As I reached the crow's nest and peeked through the opening, my entire world froze. Freda cornered June at the edge of the crow's nest, sword extended. June leaned back into the wall. Her body curved backward as she avoided another stab from Freda's sword.

Then she toppled back off the crow's nest.

"NO!" I didn't think, letting the next wave of flames erupt from my fingers. It flared around Freda, giving me the momentary reprieve to grab June's cutlass from the floor.

And shove it straight into Freda's burning body.

I made sure she kept staring at me as her life left her body with each drip of blood and charred skin. Until at last, she fell to the ground, as empty as a barrel that once held water.

With death as a new friend in the crow's nest, I raced to where June toppled over the edge. I nearly cried. She hung on the edge with one hand, face pale and eyes wide.

"Give me your arm!" I reached over the edge. She swung her bad arm up toward me, and with a grunt, I hoisted her back into the crow's nest. We toppled backward, landing beside Freda's body.

June pressed her forehead against mine, closing her eyes for a moment. If I didn't know any better, I would have thought she was crying.

As we held each other close, she whispered, "You know, I wanted to kill Freda."

I half-laughed, "Too bad your first mate is far too competent."

"Maybe you should be captain."

"Nah. That's your role, Captain Lok. You need me to keep you alive."

And as the last swords clashed and Freda's blood dried, I kissed June hard just to make sure she was alive.

CHAPTER TWENTY-SEVEN

A Funeral For Lies

C allum's casket floated out to sea as a lonesome hero surrounded by the corpses of villains. I stood in silence on the deck of the *Cobalt Hare*, with June on my left and Tristan on my right. Hari watched from the crow's nest, the wind catching her hair, while Pickford played a sad tune on his harmonica. It didn't matter that the *Cobalt Hare*'s crew had been slaughtered, with the survivors locked in the brig and the acquirees free. It didn't matter that I found my brother or that June got her revenge.

We lost a crewmate.

And we could never fill that void.

As Callum's casket passed the last corpses, Tristan and I stepped to the railing. With a single nod, we cast our fire, letting it rush across the water, and set the grave ablaze. A final goodbye, a final rest, and a final breath.

Once the flames went out, the crew diminished, disappearing below deck or back to the *Sanguine Tortuga*. June and I exchanged a single nod, then she vanished into Freda's captain's quarters while I sat on a crate next to my brother, inhaling the silence.

Tristan broke it with a half-laugh, "Can't believe you're a pirate now…"

"And I can't believe June didn't kill you."

"Why would she kill me?"

"Because you turned her into Freda."

"She asked me to."

"Point." I shook my head. Typical June.

Tristan sighed and wrung his hands together. "I can't believe Mother sold you… and fled."

After the battle, I gave him my old letters and let him read through them. Then, I wove him my tale, filling in the missing details. He called me a liar as I described the seagrip, and his interest piqued at the mention of the silver pool. If it was anyone else, I would have stopped with the discovery of my flame. But even after all these years, we were of the same womb.

"What did you think happened?" I asked.

"Honestly? I thought you both ran off. Fled to the mainland or something to avoid trouble with the law. Didn't expect her to… *sell* you."

"I guess I didn't either." I flicked my fingers, casting a temporary flame on my thumb. It rested there for a moment, only for Tristan to transfer it to his palm and sculpt it into a flower reminiscent of the one hanging around my neck.

"That's amazing..." I whispered, "I can't do that."

"Years of practice." Tristan blew on it. The flower floated into the air, then rested in the heart of my necklace. The fire flickered for a moment, then dissipated, causing the translucent petals to ripple with orange.

I placed my hand over the flower. "That was beautiful."

"I don't doubt you'll do that and more someday. Especially with a necklace like that."

"What do you mean?"

"It's magic. I can tell."

"Really?"

"You recognize things... especially when you're trained to."

I wiggled my question in with that statement. "What do you mean 'trained to'? What happened to you, Tristan?"

He sighed and closed his hands. "It's not as... fantastic as your story."

"I don't care. Tell me."

He opened his hands again, this time with a new flame in his hand. "I spent six months in prison, waiting for Mother to bail me out. Prison is...something. I...did whatever I had to, to save myself from harm. The things I did… They haunt me still. I was just a boy. But…I had to do it to survive…" He gritted his teeth.

I didn't dare ask what happened. I had my imagination, and he had his truth.

He continued, "After about six months, I paid my debt by joining the military. They loved the idea of training a pyromancer, likening me to our father and everything. It's not like I had a choice. So they took me under their wing. They even let me visit the old home… only for me to see it abandoned. After poking around, I learned you had boarded an obsidian ship by the name of the *Sanguine Tortuga*. I only assumed Mother did the same." His eyes grew distant. "I would be lying if I said I wasn't angry. You abandoned me. So I spent the next years distracted by learning about magic and how to control my flame."

"You've done a good job with it," I said.

"I did it 'cause that was all I had. Every time I mastered part of my magic, in sending flames through the sky or annihilating a target, the governor would come and praise me. I was her new pet. She kept me by her side whenever diplomats would come, just to show off that Janis was under the protection of my flame. And that's how I found out that the *Sanguine Tortuga* was taken by pirates."

"So that's why you thought I was dead?" I asked.

"I could only assume… since I knew you boarded that ship. You might have only gathered passage, but it was easier for me to just assume you were dead." He blinked a couple times, hiding the tears. "The *Cobalt Hare* brought the news after discovering some crewmates stranded on some sandbar. They were warning all the islands of June's power. So that's when I joined their crew, against the wishes of the governor."

"She let you go?"

"Once I gave her the sum that Ms. Platt offered, yes."

"So you sold yourself?"

"It was the only way to get out of that mess."

"And now you're here?"

"We weren't going to be in this location initially... but we got a message from a small El Limra fishing boat you were heading back this way. Figured to wait it out in the Vapor Pit. That way, we might corner you. Didn't expect you all to come rushing toward us, blazing with fire."

"I'm their secret weapon." I grinned at him.

"Glad you were." He nudged my shoulder.

I elbowed him back, just like when we were children sitting on the pier. We'd been stolen from each other, each suffering a different form of imprisonment while our childhoods withered away. But now, despite everything, we'd returned, two flames determined to light the way.

I returned to the *Sanguine Tortuga* with June that evening. With the *Cobalt Hare* tied to us, we drifted through the Vapor Pit, raking in our treasures. June had ransacked Freda's office, stealing four different treasure maps and a bucket of gold.

Pickford sat on a barrel as we climbed aboard, more enthralled with adjusting the binding around his chest than greeting us. Since the battle, he hadn't smiled all that much. He didn't defend Theo, and when he glimpsed Callum's casket for the first time, I thought he might lock himself in his room for a week.

Even though Callum was a quiet fellow, his death hung over the ship. Unfinished canvases waited on the deck, and above us all, his red flag with the image of a skeletal tortoise waved.

But most of all, Hari's presence reminded us of his death. As we climbed aboard, she was nowhere to be seen, though, and with a nod toward June, I disappeared below decks to check on her.

Yet she didn't wait in her room or in the galley. Her usual spots in the artillery or gangway remained empty. My heart sank, assuming the worst. She had to know that we would stand by her. Even without Callum, we were her family.

An incomprehensible shout pulled those worries from my mind. I burst into a run, pushing through the hall toward the noise.

The scream waited for me in the brig, where Hari stood holding Theo by the collar of his shirt. A bruise tarnished his forehead with black and blue.

"Now tell me, why did you lead us here?!" she yelled at him.

Theo stared past her, dejection in his eyes, and no answers on his lips.

"Tell me!" She pulled him forward, slamming his head against the bars.

"Hari! Wait!"

She glowered at me. "Stay out of this, Leena!"

"You're going to kill him! Then you'll never get your answer!"

"I don't care!"

"Hari!"

Hari huffed and dropped him. Theo's small body fell to the ground like a rag doll. He lifted his head to stare at me but still didn't speak.

"Then what do you suppose we do? He killed Callum!" Tears formed in Hari's eyes. "He killed him…"

"I know." I approached Theo's cell and knelt before it. Our eyes locked. Slowly, I spoke, "Theo, I would like to thank you for leading me to my brother."

He perked up slightly.

"But this is not how I wanted to find him. Now, one of our crewmates is dead. Why is that?"

Theo licked his lips.

"I recommend you tell me."

He still didn't speak.

"Very well," I sighed. Then, with my fire rushing through me, I slammed my hand through the bars of the cell. A single flame ignited on my index finger, and without flinching, I jammed that finger straight into his eye.

He fell backward, a blood-curdling scream escaping his lips as he rolled over on the floor.

"Now speak," I ordered.

He held his face in his hands as he spoke. "I had to."

"No. You chose to. Why?"

He squirmed.

"Answer me!" I sent a flame through the bars. It skidded over Theo's head, burning a few strands of hair.

He gasped out, tears deep in his voice, "I had to stop it…"

"Stop what?"

"The war…"

"What?"

"If you trade the silver liquid, war will come. I had to stop it. We can't let that war happen… we can't…"

"Theo…" I shook my head, staring down at him. "The trade already happened. You did this for nothing."

"No… not that… the future…"

Hari interjected, "The future is indefinite. You've said that before, Theo. And now Callum is dead because of it."

"I didn't see that outcome. I'm sorry."

"What did you see then?" Hari's entire body shook as she questioned him.

"I—"

"Answer her," I ordered.

Theo closed his remaining eye. "I saw nothing."

"So, why did you take us here?"

"Because it was the only option with no definitive future."

Hari threw herself at the bars, tears falling from her face as she screamed, "You chose an indefinite future over the lives of your friends!? What were you thinking!?"

Theo didn't reply.

"Did you think you'd be some great hero for stopping some… some nonexistent war!? You could have talked to us, Theo!"

"You think June would have listened?"

"She would have respected your thoughts!" I intervened. "She's not evil."

"She is a pirate."

I leaned forward, the warmth once again rippling through my hands. "Theo... we're all pirates here. And if there's one thing that I've learned about piracy, it's that the crew sticks together."

Theo locked his one remaining eye with my eye. At that moment, he understood. He locked his future the moment he betrayed us.

He had been my friend. My brother, in a way.

But he tested my patience, and now... Callum was dead. Hari was aching.

Sure, I reunited with my brother, but at what cost?

I wouldn't kill Theo. I didn't have that in my heart.

But I could take the last thing he held dear.

So with one last movement, I thrust my hand into his cell.

And burned out his other eye.

I found June in her quarters, poring over the maps she'd taken from the *Cobalt Hare*. Blood dripped from my hands as I entered her cabin. She didn't flinch as I sat down in front of her, enthralled with the maps, a smirk on her lips.

"Freda had all these maps! We're gonna find so many treasures..." June raised her eyes. "What's with the blood?"

"Dealt with Theo," I muttered.

"You kill him?"

"No. Worse." I picked at my nail. "I took away his sight."

"A seer without sight. Better than I would have done." June leaned back in her seat. "Proud of you, Leena. You've come a long way."

"Learned from the best."

"Good. It means you'll make a great captain."

"What do you mean?"

"I wanna give you the *Cobalt Hare*. You deserve it."

My heart lurched. My own ship? I never fathomed being a captain. It was a high honor, without a doubt, promoted to captain of our first conquered ship. But...

"I don't want it," I said to her. "That's not my crew."

"Think about it, Leena! The two of us could rule the seas with these obsidian ships." June took my bloodied hands. "People would fear our every move."

"We're better together, not apart." I didn't dare tell her how much I would miss her. The idea of sailing off on my own held no appeal. Without June by my side, I would be no captain. We were a team, and together, we could rule the seas.

Not apart.

Not alone.

"Leena, I can only trust you to take this ship. I can't be in two places at once."

"I know. But I don't want it. Give it to someone else."

"No one else deserves it. Not like you."

"There are others…" I squeezed her hands. "Please. I want to stay aboard this ship… *our* ship. Please."

She stroked my hand. "Then I give you the ship, and you can give it away to someone. Who do you trust to lead the *Cobalt Hare*?"

I peered toward the window, the weight of Theo's blood on my hands, and countless deaths on my shoulders. There was only one person I would ever trust with my life. Even after all this time, I trusted he would care for that ship with his full heart and soul.

"Simple," I said to June. "We give it to my brother."

CHAPTER TWENTY-EIGHT

Adventure Bathed in Red

We offered the *Cobalt Hare* to my brother the next morning. He paced the deck of the ship, observing each of its pillars, a contemplative expression on his face that I recognized from our childhood. He ran his finger along the burnt mast of the crow's nest, then glanced behind him at a few members of the *Cobalt Hare*'s crew.

"So I guess... you won't be coming with me?" he asked.

"This is my life now, Tristan. Maybe a few months ago... yeah, I would have. But..." I brushed my fingers over June's hand as she stood beside me. "This is where I belong."

"Ever thought I might want to join your crew?"

"Do you?" My heart almost leapt.

But I already knew his answer.

"Ha. No. You might have abandoned your morals, but I still have some."

"I didn't abandon my morals. They merely... changed."

Tristan scoffed. His attention fell on the captain's cabin at the back of the ship. "I imagine if I take this that there is a contingency, right?"

"Smart. I like him," June said to me.

"Yeah, he's a little too smart." I laughed.

June then turned to Tristan, "Help us establish a trade route in the north. We got some valuable goods, and if we get their support, we'll rule these seas."

"What's my cut?" Tristan asked.

"You're getting a ship."

"I'll need money to keep it financed... and to keep this crew happy. Doubt all of them will be too enthused."

"They seem fine now."

"Only because they're scared of you."

June leaned back on her heels and exhaled. "Fine. Twenty percent."

"Fifty."

"Thirty-five."

"Forty."

"Fine."

Tristan smirked, but there remained that hesitancy in his gaze. He stepped toward the captain's cabin and stroked the doorknob with his fingers. Sparks flew as he touched it. "I didn't join this ship planning to climb the ranks or anything. Always thought I'd go back to Janis and continue to serve the governor."

"Is that what you want to do?" I asked.

He gripped the doorknob. "No… not at all."

"So… you accept?"

He twisted the knob. "If my crew wrings my neck, then I'll haunt you from beyond the grave."

"Oh, come on, at this rate, I'm dying way before you." I chided.

"We'll see." He winked and opened the captain's door.

After being tethered together for nearly a week, we faced the last day with the *Cobalt Hare*. Pickford helped me load one of our two remaining barrels of silver liquid onto the ship, securing it deep within the hull of the ship. Tristan knew the story of our discovery, and with that, he would take it north to find us more traders and secure our position in the sea.

"Are you okay?" I asked Pickford as we loaded the barrel on board.

"Hm? Yeah, of course."

"Even with everything that happened to Theo?"

Pickford smiled, "Yeah, it's fine. Brat deserved what he got."

"You were his friend. Are you sure?"

"Weren't you also his friend?"

I didn't reply.

Pickford secured the ropes, not looking at me. "Went down to the brig a few times. Theo seems more at peace now than ever before if you want to know the truth. All those visions overwhelmed him. Now he can just... exist."

I checked the knot. "His sight was a burden on us all."

"It got us out of a few predicaments."

"But is that worth the life of a friend?"

"Yeah, that is the question." Pickford brushed back his hair and removed a piece of chocolate from his coat pocket. "I'm gonna miss that little guy. He was annoying but a good kid."

I nodded. Silently, we climbed up the ladder to the main deck, wearing Callum's name like a heavy badge in our hearts. We didn't need to say his name. His presence would weigh on us as the flag of the *Sanguine Tortuga* flittered against the wind.

We joined June on deck, where she spoke to my brother, arms crossed. My brother stood his own against her, his hands in his pockets. He took in each word with that thoughtfulness that I remembered. While I hadn't witnessed it, I trusted he had already assembled his crew, putting together with finesse the best way to operate the ship. I had not a doubt in my mind that he would herald this ship with the same care.

The sound of someone approaching from behind caused me to turn. Hari grimaced at me, a bag over her shoulder, eyes downcast.

"Hari!" I exclaimed. "It's good to see you in daylight!"

"I did miss the sun," she whispered, adjusting the bag on her shoulder.

My heart sank. "You're leaving, aren't you?"

She nodded. "I can't stay on the *Sanguine Tortuga*. Not after everything that happened." Tears filled her eyes, but she blinked them away. "Honestly, Callum might have been the only thing keeping me there. After the way Hackney treated me... and all the death and blood spilled... I can't do it."

"Where will you go?"

"Perhaps back to Jrin Ayl... or somewhere else. Really, I haven't decided. I'm sure the *Cobalt Hare* will take me there, though."

I understood. Of course I did. If June had died, would I have stayed aboard the *Sanguine Tortuga*?

Or would I have sought vengeance across the sea?

But Callum's killer was dead. Theo's eyes were gone. What else could she do?

What would Callum want?

"I hope we'll meet again someday," I said to her.

"I hope so too. Take care of yourself, Leena. Don't get into too much trouble, alright?"

"Eh. That's no fun."

She almost laughed, pulling me into a one-arm hug. I leaned into her. It would be strange not having her on board; she had been such a good friend and confidante. Over the years, we might have grown further apart, but we were still sisters in the end.

"Take care of my brother for me." I sniffled, holding back my tears.

"If I could handle you and June, I'm pretty sure I can handle him." She squeezed me one more time, then we released, each stepping back to go our separate ways.

I suppose I should have known how much everything might change. But already, the emptiness left behind by Hari's departure nestled into my stomach. Sure, there would be new crewmates, but with her and Callum gone, something would always be missing onboard the *Sanguine Tortuga*.

But as one hole opens in the heart, another closes.

My brother approached me, wearing a captain's uniform and a comprehensive belt hitched with a sword, spyglass, and other such items. We said not a word. Everything had been said. Now, our future was as endless as the sea.

We had found our way back to each other, but blue painted his path while mine was bathed in red. Our destinies, entwined forever, would diverge until we would meet again, as fate inevitably decreed.

"June asked I rendezvous with you all to the Vapor Pit in a year's time. You think you can stay alive until then?" He asked.

"I've been living this life for years. Do you think *you'll* stay alive?"

"Guess we'll see." He grinned at me, then his face softened. He removed an object from his belt and unfurled it.

My old wooden sword greeted me.

"You got the sword!" I said, laughing.

"Had to bring it back to you." He handed it to me. "Please don't get into too much trouble, Leena. Truly."

I took the sword and held it tight. "I can't make any promises."

Laughing, we embraced, hugging tight for a long moment. Years ago, returning to my brother meant securing our lives together, never to be torn apart. Now, I had a different future, a different path, and a different ship.

And I wouldn't trade it for anything.

From the crow's nest, I watched as the *Cobalt Hare* disappeared on the horizon, holding my old wooden sword close to my side. The identical twin to the *Sanguine Tortuga*, its blue obsidian exterior glistened in the late afternoon light as it headed north. I could only imagine what Tristan and Hari were up to on deck. Was Hari simply sitting in her room, or had she taken up a temporary position as quartermaster onboard? Did Tristan mingle with his crew? Or did he go down below to observe the strange silver liquid we thrust upon him?

And what of their crew? I hadn't talked to most of them, but like us, they were all acquirees, stolen from their home. What sort of life would they live now?

"Knock, knock." June stuck her head up into the crow's nest. "Am I allowed up here?"

"June!" I ran to help her into the crow's nest. "What're you doing up here?"

"Aren't I allowed to spend time with my first mate?"

"But you're scared of heights!"

"Not anymore… at least not if you're by my side."

I grinned at her, taking her hand and raising it to my lips.

"So, why are you up here all alone?" She asked.

"Just watching the *Cobalt Hare* leave."

"Do you regret not taking it?"

"Absolutely not." I squeezed her hand, redirecting my attention so it fell only on her face. "This is my ship, and I am your first mate. I'm not going anywhere."

"Good." June leaned into me. "Because otherwise, there's no point in heading to Janis."

"We're still heading to Janis?"

"Of course… why wouldn't we? I thought you wanted to go home."

I laughed. "June, I've already been home. I've been home for a while."

"Then where do you want to go?" she asked.

I glanced over her toward the sea, glistening in hues of sanguine red. The world beckoned us, calling for the next adventure and the next treasure. We had no rules, no plan, and no destination.

We didn't need any.

Because the tides could take us anywhere, and the sea would always be our home.

The adventure continues in...

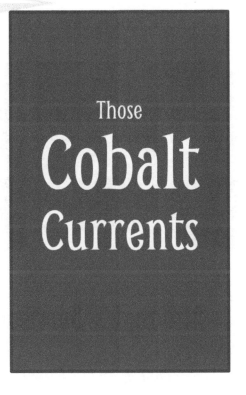

Those
Cobalt
Currents

Coming Late 2024

Want more stories from the Effluvium?

Check out...

  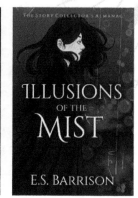

Also by E.S. Barrison

The Life & Death Cycle
The Story Collector's Almanac
The Unsought Fairy Tale Collection

Author's Note

Dear Reader,

I would like to take the time to thank you.

Thank you for picking up this book.

Thank you for joining me on this adventure.

And thank you for letting me share a part of me with you.

These Sanguine Tides, in some ways, is the first story that made me realize "yes, I want to be an author." While the story I wrote at the age of eleven in no way resembles what is on the page today, I cannot deny its impact.

That story, like this one, told the tale of two siblings who both shared fire magic. Their names have since changed, as has the plot. Eleven-year-old me would not recognize this story and that's okay.

But for those of you who are inspired to write, my words to you are this: keep writing. With each word, you'll not only become a stronger writer, but discover more of yourself.

With each book, I've discovered more of myself as well. That never stops. Your characters take a piece of you and run with it on the page.

Leena was no different.

So I hope that her story resonated with you as well.

If it did, then I hope you'll consider sharing this story with others. Whether by word of mouth, or leaving an online review, every person you tell helps this story reach a larger audience.

So once again, thank you and I hope to see you on more adventures in the World of the Effluvium.

E.S. Barrison

About the Author

E.S. Barrison has been writing and creating stories for as long as she can remember. After graduating from the University of Florida, she has spent the past few years wrangling her experiences to compose unique worlds with diverse characters. Currently, E.S. lives in Orlando, Florida with her family.

www.esbarrison-author.com

Ingram Content Group UK Ltd.
Milton Keynes UK
UKHW021028300323
419408UK00016B/1098